At the

D0760597

"The best Regency romanc

—Pam Rosenthal, RITA-Award winning Author

"The perfect summer read! Four fabulous authors in one place!"

—Sarah MacLean, *NYT* Bestselling Author

"Filled with romance, passion, danger, scandal, and love … A must-read!"

—*My Book Addiction and More*

"A delightful anthology. The four stories are tied together wonderfully … entertaining, fun and heartwarming."

—*Romance Novel News*

Praise for *When I Met My Duchess*

"Linden's *When I Met My Duchess* is the standout star."

—*RT BookReviews* on *At the Duke's Wedding*

WHEN I MET MY DUCHESS

CAROLINE LINDEN

Caroline Linden

BOOKS BY CAROLINE LINDEN

ISBN-10: 0-9971494-6-9

ISBN-13: 978-0-9971494-6-3

To Tarka

ABOUT THIS STORY

When I Met My Duchess was originally published as part of the anthology *At The Duke's Wedding*, featuring wonderful stories by Maya Rodale, Miranda Neville, and Katharine Ashe. If you'd like to read more about Jack Willoughby and his magnificent phaeton, discover what brought the Earl of Bruton to duel with his cousin, and learn just who the mysterious Angela is and why she's staying with Sophronia, *At The Duke's Wedding* is available from online retailers and in print.

And don't miss the sequel, also set at Kingstag Castle, called *At the Christmas Wedding*.

I t was going to be a terrific storm.

Gareth Cavendish, Duke of Wessex, surveyed the rapidly darkening sky as he stood on the steps of his country estate. Gray-violet clouds boiled up in angry billows and every few seconds thunder rumbled, as if the storm were clearing its throat, preparing to roar. But so far not a drop had fallen.

"I do hope they're near," he murmured, scanning the pristine landscape of his property. "The clouds may burst at any moment."

The man behind him shifted his weight. "Sir William is a very punctual man."

"Yes." Gareth narrowed his gaze upon a far-off puff of dust, just visible beyond the stately oaks that lined the road leading to Kingstag Castle. A servant had been sent out to watch for the visitors' arrival, but it was still over a mile from the main gates to the house. A moment later, a traveling chaise-and-four emerged around the last turn. "There. Just as you said, Blair. Very punctual."

His secretary murmured a vague reply.

The carriage bowled smartly down the drive, drawing

nearer. He stood a little straighter. It wasn't every day a man welcomed his bride-to-be to his home. Miss Helen Grey, younger daughter of Sir William Grey and the toast of the Season, would be the Duchess of Wessex by the end of the month. Gareth was very pleased with the match. Her father's best property marched with one of his smaller estates, and according to the marriage settlements, that land would be his one day, as Grey had no sons. It was a good match as well, for the Greys were an old and respected family, even if they had fallen on rather hard times of late. And the young lady herself was ideal: a serene, gracious manner, a lovely face and form, and a beautiful voice. Helen Grey would make the perfect Duchess of Wessex.

Gareth glanced again at the sky. He hoped the storm broke soon and blew over quickly. Guests were to begin arriving the next day, and he shuddered to imagine the chaos if everyone was kept indoors for the next week.

"Let us hope there are no lightning strikes, hmm?" He half-turned to flash a faint smile at his secretary, who nodded, stony-faced. Gareth took another look at the man who was not merely his secretary. James Blair was his distant cousin from a poorer branch of the family and superbly competent. He relied on him like he relied on his right arm. Normally they worked together in perfect tandem, Blair anticipating his thoughts and Gareth relying on his cousin's uncommonly good judgment in all matters. No one was more closely acquainted with his business concerns or personal matters, nor a better friend. He trusted the man completely.

But now his secretary looked as though a funeral train were approaching instead of a bridal party. "All right, Blair?" he asked curiously.

Blair stared straight ahead, his eyes flat. "Yes."

He glanced toward the approaching chaise as an awful thought struck him. Good Lord. There couldn't be something about this marriage giving him pause, could there? Blair had conducted the marriage settlement negotiations on his behalf while estate business had kept Gareth in the country. Naturally, he must have seen Miss Grey and her family a fair amount. Alarm stirred in his chest. Perhaps Blair has seen something troubling but hesitated to bring it up now that the documents had been signed and the engagement announced. Blair would notice. Blair also would not want to embarrass him.

He cleared his throat. "You seem quiet. No reservations about the bride, I hope?"

At last Blair looked at him, albeit reluctantly. "No. Miss Grey is a very suitable choice."

That seemed an evasive answer. "Were there any problems with Sir William?" he asked, lowering his voice even further. Blair shook his head. "Come, man, what is it?" he prodded. "You look positively grim."

Blair's chest filled as if he would speak, and then he sighed. "My apologies, Wessex," he muttered. "It must be the storm."

Gareth closed his eyes and mentally smacked himself on the forehead; he'd completely forgotten Blair had been frightened of storms as a boy. Perhaps he still was, and now Gareth had just gone and forced him to admit it aloud. "Of course," he murmured quickly.

"I wish you and Miss Grey every happiness," added his secretary with a forced smile.

Gareth nodded, happy to let the conversation lapse. The carriage was almost to the steps, and for a second he wondered what he might have done if Blair had confessed some wariness about Miss Grey or the marriage in general. He couldn't very well just send her home, but it would have been gravely alarming had James found her wanting.

There was a rustle of silk behind him. "I hope I'm not late," said his mother as she stepped up beside him.

"Your timing is perfect," he said. "I presume Bridget had something to do with it."

"As ever," she replied under her breath.

Gareth shot his mother a quick glance. All three of his sisters were beside themselves with excitement over the impending celebrations and desperately eager to meet Miss Grey, the reigning toast of London. But while Serena and Alexandra were capable of proper, dignified behavior, the youngest had a true genius for trouble. If anything were to break, go missing, or inexplicably wind up on the roof, Bridget was sure to be found nearby, protesting—with a perfectly straight face—that the most incredible circum-stances had caused it. Normally he took Bridget's mishaps in stride, but he would be eternally grateful if she managed to behave properly for the next fortnight. Perhaps he ought to tell Withers, the butler, to post footmen outside the guest rooms to make certain Bridget didn't accidentally inflict a broken leg or a black eye on the bride.

"She'll be on her best behavior, won't she?" he asked, praying that would be good enough.

"Yes." The duchess gave him a confident smile. "I've told her she will be excluded from all the wedding festivities if she is not. For now, I've sent her to help Henrietta entertain Sophronia."

His shoulders eased. "A masterstroke." The only person more capable than Bridget of causing trouble was Sophronia, his great-great-aunt. Or was she a great-great-great-aunt? He tended to think of her in the same vein as the statues in the garden: ancient, crumbling, and utterly impervious to anything. Normally Sophronia kept to her own apartments with her companion, Henrietta Black, but if she and Bridget could occupy each other tonight, so much the better for everyone.

"Never let it be said I don't know my children." His

mother turned to face him and her gaze sharpened. "Do you love this girl, Gareth?"

She only called him Gareth when she wanted to get his attention. His eyes narrowed, but he spoke calmly. "What has love got to do with marriage?" He knew it existed and that it was pleasant to find it in marriage, but he'd never met a woman who stirred him, even slightly, the way poets and romantics sighed about: the world upended, walking on air, being struck by lightning from a clear blue sky. Rubbish. Whatever else Gareth might have been amenable to, he preferred to keep his feet on the ground, and he most certainly didn't want to be hit by lightning. If such a force even existed, he was just as happy not to know about it. His marriage to Miss Grey would be elegant, refined, and sensible: in a word, perfect.

"Don't scoff," said his parent. "You know I only ask out of concern. You've persuaded me the match is advantageous for both parties, but you've hardly said one word about your feelings for the lady herself."

"She's lovely. She'll make a very suitable duchess and mother. You'll adore her."

"I wasn't worried about adoring her myself," replied the duchess. "I worry about *you* adoring her."

His jaw tightened. What a time to ask that question. "I have the utmost respect for her, and I trust we shall be very content with one another."

His mother only sighed.

Irked at her and at Blair for ruffling what had promised to be a perfectly smooth welcoming, he descended the steps as the carriage reached the gravel and slowed to a more decorous speed. There was nothing to reproach in his actions. He was a sensible man who made logical decisions. He thought he'd chosen quite well, despite his mother's sentimental disquiet and his secretary's grim silence. If they had some objection to this marriage, he thought darkly, they had better speak soon or forever hold their peace.

But this was not the moment to brood about that. Straightening his shoulders, he prepared to welcome his future wife and her family. Miss Grey, her parents, and her elder sister would spend the next fortnight at Kingstag, preparing for the wedding at the end of that time. Behind him, the butler, housekeeper, and a few servants waited at the ready to greet their soon-to-be mistress. The house had been cleaned and polished to a bright shine over the last month to appear at its best for the wedding. He darted a quick glance at his mother, but she silently stepped up beside him, her serene smile back in place, and he breathed a sigh of relief.

The sky growled again as the coach pulled to a halt. A dust-covered servant jumped down to open the door, and Sir William alighted first. The baronet fairly radiated triumph. "A very great pleasure, Your Grace," he boomed, sweeping a bow as the servant turned to help Lady Grey down.

"The pleasure is mine, sir. Welcome." Gareth greeted the older gentleman. "May I present my mother, the Duchess of Wessex?" His mother stepped forward and graciously greeted the baronet.

Gareth turned his attention to Lady Grey. "Welcome to Kingstag Castle, madam." He bowed over her hand.

Her pleased eyes climbed the façade of the house before she turned a beaming smile on him. "A pleasure it is to be here, sir. And for such a happy occasion!" She laughed, a little trill of delight. He smiled, then stepped forward to help his betrothed down from the carriage himself.

Helen Grey was lovely, he thought approvingly as she stepped down, her small hand nestled in his. He'd thought so from the moment he met her. Her dark hair was arranged in the latest style, her dress the picture of elegance. She looked as fresh and beautiful as the roses in his mother's garden. The Greys must have stopped so she could change and refresh herself before arriving. "Welcome to my home, Miss Grey." He raised her hand to his lips as he bowed.

She blushed, her cheeks a perfect soft pink. Her dark eyes glowed as she gave a little curtsey. "Thank you, Your Grace. I'm delighted to arrive at last."

Gareth smiled in satisfaction. She truly was the perfect bride. Her voice was just as lovely as he remembered, and her person even lovelier. Her manner was gentle and sweet. What more could a man ask for in a wife? He presented her to the duchess, pleased to see his mother greet her as warmly and graciously as ever. He knew she would never be rude or crass, but he wouldn't put it past her to probe—in that delicate, almost imperceptible way she had—into Miss Grey's feelings as well.

"How fortunate you arrived before the storm broke," he said to Sir William. "It's been threatening all day."

"Yes!" exclaimed Lady Grey, fanning herself. "We were quite worried we would be caught in a downpour."

"It looks to be a bad one," observed Sir William, squinting at the sky.

"Indeed. Shall we proceed inside?" Gareth paused, remembering something. "But did you not say your eldest daughter would also be accompanying you?"

A moment of silence passed over the group. Sir William and Lady Grey exchanged a glance. Miss Grey wet her lips. "Yes. My sister did come. She wanted a moment to repair her appearance, I believe."

"Ah." Gareth nodded, and turned toward the carriage again, wishing the sister would hurry up and get down so they could step inside before the rain came and soaked them all. How long did she need to repair herself, anyway? Miss Grey managed to look as neat and elegant as any lady in town.

"I'm coming," said a voice from the carriage. "Just a moment!" She appeared in the door of the carriage, her face hidden by a dark red bonnet. She gathered up her vibrant yellow skirt in one hand and reached out to take the hand of the footman waiting to assist her. "So sorry to keep everyone waiting," she said a bit breathlessly as she jumped down and faced them all.

She looked like her sister, but different. Where Helen Grey's face was tranquil and composed, this woman's face was lively and expressive. Her eyes sparkled and danced. Her features were sharper than Helen's and her figure was fuller, almost lush. And as she tipped up her pointed chin and looked at Gareth with openly interested brown eyes, lightning struck.

Everyone jumped at the thunderous crash and the burst of light that burned a streak across the sky. "Gracious!" cried Lady Grey, clapping a hand to her heart. "I thought it would strike us all dead on the spot!"

Helen's sister turned her face to the sky as the first sharp drops of rain hit the ground. "It looks to be a good show," she said mischievously.

"Indeed not, Cleo," said her mother in an undertone. "Behave yourself!"

Gareth heard all this dimly, around the introduction. Mrs. Cleopatra Barrows, Sir William was saying, his eldest daughter. He thought he made the polite response but couldn't be sure; once he took her gloved hand in his, he wasn't quite sure what else went on in the world around him. It wouldn't surprise him if his hair were standing on end, and he was most likely staring like an idiot. Mrs. Barrows put on a polite smile and curtseyed, but that excitement that sprang into her face at the crack of lightning stuck in his mind.

A soft noise behind him finally broke whatever spell he'd fallen under. He stepped back, remembering himself. "I'm delighted you've arrived at last. You remember Mr. Blair, of course?" Blair stepped forward and bowed.

"Capital to see you, sir," said Sir William courteously, and Lady Grey gave him a benevolent smile.

"Mr. Blair," murmured Miss Grey.

"Mrs. Barrows," said the duchess, coming toward her. "What a delight to make your acquaintance. Welcome to Kingstag Castle."

"Thank you, Your Grace." She dropped a graceful curtsy.

"And you must meet Mr. Blair," his mother continued, looking at Blair, who obediently stepped to her side. "He is Wessex's secretary as well as our cousin."

"How do you do, sir?" Mrs. Barrows gave Blair a sunny smile, and Gareth's stomach clenched. He had to make himself turn away from her, unnerved by his reaction.

"Come, let us go inside," he said, offering Lady Grey his arm. "The guests will begin arriving tomorrow. I thought you might like a day to explore the castle on your own before they lay siege to the place."

Lady Grey gave her trilling little laugh again as she fell in step beside him. "How kind of you to arrange it so, sir! We are thoroughly delighted to be invited for such a stay, and to meet your mother and sisters! I vow, Kingstag Castle is every bit as lovely as I'd heard . . ."

She chattered on as they walked inside. Gareth was aware of Mrs. Barrows walking behind him with Blair. In the doorway he stole a glance back, catching sight of his cousin's smile at something she said. Miss Grey followed, listening soberly to his mother, but her sister chatted quite amiably with Blair.

He felt a strange stab of discontent in his chest. Logically, he should hope Mrs. Barrows could revive Blair from whatever melancholy he'd sunk into lately. He should hope his cousin took a great enough liking to Mrs. Barrows to entertain her for the next fortnight, leaving Miss Grey to him.

Somehow, he didn't.

The housekeeper stepped forward to show the guests to their rooms to refresh themselves and rest. Although, as Mrs. Barrows passed him with a swish of her brilliant skirt, he couldn't help but think that the Greys didn't look in great need of refreshing. Gareth watched as they climbed the stairs, Lady Grey in the lead with the housekeeper and his mother, followed by Miss Grey and Mrs. Barrows.

"Just as lovely as you remembered?" asked Blair quietly, coming up beside him.

Gareth tore his gaze off Mrs. Barrows's figure, trying to shake off the unpleasant feeling of having been knocked sideways. "Yes."

Blair exhaled. He still looked a little ill, his mouth tight and his eyes shadowed. "That is a great relief."

Gareth breathed deeply. The ladies had reached the turn of the stairs, and he watched Mrs. Barrows trail one gloved hand along the banister appreciatively. "Yes. It is, isn't it? I can hardly stop the marriage now."

Blair shook his head slowly, still watching the women climb the stairs. "No. I don't suppose you can."

"Gracious, Helen, you never said he was so handsome!"

Cleo burst into her sister's room, too full of energy to rest. Helen was lying obediently on the bed, but at Cleo's entrance she sat up at once, just as she had since they were girls. Of course, this time their nurse wouldn't come scold them for not resting like proper young ladies, thought Cleo with a grin, since she was a widowed lady and her sister was about to become a duchess.

"Do you really think so?" Helen's face lit up with a luminous smile.

Cleo laughed. "Of course! Such broad shoulders! Such brooding eyes! Such a lovely home!" She laughed again. "Did

Mama see Kingstag Castle before you accepted his offer, or after? I thought she would swoon with delight when the house came into view."

Helen sighed, her glow fading. "After. You well know she would have liked him had the house been a fright. He's a duke, Cleo, and very wealthy," she said in perfect imitation of their mother's voice. "What more does a girl want?"

"Mmm, and handsome, too," Cleo added. "A mother might want a title and a fortune, but a girl wants a handsome face."

Helen tried, and failed, to repress her grin. "Cleo, you're wicked."

"Of course I am," she exclaimed. "That's why you love to have me about. But hush—" She lowered her voice and glanced around. "I did promise to be on my best behavior this fortnight," she whispered. "So you mustn't let on when I'm my usual awful self, or Papa will send me packing."

Helen's smile disappeared. "It was dreadful that Papa said that to you," she said in a low tone. "You are not awful."

Cleo lifted one shoulder. "To them I am. The stench of trade, you know. I suppose someday I might give away all my money and take up embroidery or some other suitable pursuit and live out my days in respectable poverty." She gave a theatrical sigh and collapsed backward on the chaise as if in a swoon, throwing up one arm over her head in a fit of drama. "Perhaps then I'll be acceptable. Poor and dull, but acceptable."

"You could never be dull," said her sister. "I'm ever so glad you've come, because if you're here, at least it won't be dull." She shuddered.

Cleo uncovered her face and looked at Helen curiously. "Do you think it will be? Why? You're reunited at last with your betrothed husband, about to meet his family and become his wife."

Helen rolled her lower lip between her teeth and plucked

at the lace on her sleeve. "I don't know him that well, Cleo," she confessed. "I've only seen him a few times this year. And last year . . . well, he didn't distinguish himself from my other suitors in any real way. It seems odd, doesn't it, that I'm to marry him in two weeks' time and I barely know his name."

"Gareth Anthony Michael Cavendish," said Cleo. "How could you not know his name, when Mama's been practicing saying it every day? *Their Graces, the Duke and Duchess of Wessex*," she mimicked her mother, just as well as Helen had done. "'Wessex of Kingstag Castle.' 'My son-in-law, the duke.' 'My daughter, the Duchess of Wessex.'"

Helen laughed again. "Stop! Perhaps I do know his name, but otherwise . . ." She shook her head. "The wedding just seems so near, all of a sudden."

This time Cleo looked more closely at her sister. It had been clear to her that Helen was nervous their entire journey, but she'd thought it was only bridal nerves. Helen wasn't usually a nervous sort, though. "Don't you want to marry him?"

Her sister's face turned bright pink. "Of course. Who would not?"

Cleo couldn't argue with that, and yet . . . "Perhaps he invited us early to get to know you better," she suggested. "To steal away into the garden with you and kiss you senseless." Helen's eyes went wide. Cleo grinned, trying to lighten the mood. "Oh, don't be like that. It's not at all a trial to be whisked into the shrubbery for a clandestine kiss from a handsome man."

Helen's smile was a trifle wistful. "Isn't it?"

"No doubt you'll soon find out." Cleo leaned forward, unable to resist prying a little. She didn't see her sister very much anymore, and she missed her. She and Helen had never had secrets from each other, once upon a time, before Cleo's marriage and subsequent widowhood had horrified her parents and made visits to the family home uncomfortable. "Don't you want him to?"

Before Helen could answer, there was a tap on the door, closely followed by the entrance of their mother. "Oh, girls," she whispered in ecstasy. "Isn't this the loveliest house? Isn't His Grace the handsomest gentleman? Oh, Helen, my darling, you are a very, very lucky girl!" She bustled over to kiss Helen's forehead. Watching her sister, Cleo thought there was a flicker of panic in Helen's eyes before she smiled at their mother.

"Thank you, Mama. I thought you were resting."

Millicent Grey waved a hand. "Pooh! As if I could sleep away my first hours at Kingstag Castle. It's one of the most beautiful estates in all of England! And my daughter will be mistress of it in just a few days' time!" She swept Helen into another embrace. Cleo draped her arms over the end of the chaise and rested her chin on her arms, watching. It had been a long time since she'd seen such an outpouring of maternal affection.

"Now, are you feeling well?" Millicent placed her hand on Helen's forehead. "Shall I send for a tonic? Luckily we've brought our own Rivers, I can have her prepare my special tonic at once."

Helen clasped her mother's wrist and smiled. "I'm fine, Mama. I don't need a tonic."

"A bath?" pressed Millicent. "I wager the duke's staff can have one ready in no time. I hear he even had pipes installed to bring in the water! Have you ever heard of such a thing? Let's send for a bath and find out."

Cleo couldn't resist rolling her eyes. Hadn't they just stopped at an inn barely three miles distant so Helen could wash and change her dress? Of course she must look lovely for her future husband—Cleo didn't argue with that—but this was silly, pretending to rest when none of them could close their eyes and wanting a bath just to discover if there really were pipes for the water.

"I'm fine, Mama." Helen pushed her mother's hand away and dodged it when Millicent would have reached out to smooth her hair. "Really, I'm quite recovered from the trip. Cleo and I were just talking about the duke."

Millicent paused, clearly caught between the excitement of gossiping about their host and wariness of whatever Cleo might have said. "Indeed?" she asked with a too-bright smile. "What did you decide?"

"That he's a very handsome gentleman," said Cleo dutifully.

"Of course he is!" Their mother beamed, relieved.

"But Helen doesn't know him all that well, does she?" Cleo went on, unable to ignore the devil inside her. "How long was his courtship?"

Millicent glared daggers at her. "It was all very proper," she said sternly. "He contacted your father, most properly, and made a very pretty proposal—"

"Before he'd spoken to Helen?" Cleo was genuinely shocked —she hadn't known that—and looked to Helen for confirmation. Her sister frowned and looked down, picking at her sleeve again.

"And his secretary—no, his *cousin*, Mr. Blair, came every week to pay his respects and make the arrangements!" Millicent lifted her chin.

"Didn't His Grace call on you, Helen?" Cleo asked, ignoring her mother.

Helen said nothing.

"Of course he did!" said Millicent indignantly. "Last Season! Several times! And twice this year!"

This was all news to Cleo. When Helen had said she didn't know the Duke of Wessex well, Cleo had thought it was due to a short but typical courtship, not one conducted by proxy. "And he sent his cousin to *propose*?"

"He did—That is—Not everyone must run wild and elope like you did, miss!" Millicent's temper got away from her, and Cleo could almost see smoke coming from her mother's ears. Behind Millicent, her sister was ripping the lace from her sleeve, her head bent.

She relented. Helen had accepted Wessex's marriage proposal, and it was her choice. She said she was happy to be marrying him. Cleo had no right to make her sister more nervous than she already was.

"No, Mama," she said soothingly. "They mustn't. And I am very happy for Helen."

Millicent opened her mouth, then closed it, as if she'd been ready for more argument. "Of course you are," she finally said, accepting the truce. "We all are. But Helen! You must rest!" Cleo watched her mother press Helen back down, fluttering around her like an excited bird. This must be a dream come to life for Millicent, marrying her most beautiful daughter to a duke, especially after the disappointment Cleo had been.

She wondered if her mother had ever had the same hopes for her, before she proved herself difficult and rebellious. She wasn't *completely* unlike Helen. She was pretty enough, though not beautiful like her sister. She'd been told she was intelligent and clever, but with an appalling tendency to speak too strongly and be too opinionated.

Her great failing, though, had been her willingness to marry a man in trade, thereby drawing shame and discredit upon all her family. Millicent, the daughter of a squire and wife of a baronet, had dreamt of having a titled son-in-law her whole life. For Cleo to saddle her with a merchant son-in-law was intolerable.

Of course, her mother's reaction to her marriage had been kind and warm compared to her father's response.

From across the room, Helen's eyes met hers, reluctantly amused and resigned. She'd always been the obedient daughter, and today was no different. Cleo would have wagered a guinea Helen would end up taking both a nap and a bath to please their mother.

She jumped to her feet. "I'm going to take a walk in the garden." It might not be the nicest thing to leave Helen at their mother's mercy, but she didn't think she could take all the smothering maternal affection. She whisked out the door and back to her own room for a shawl, then went in search of the outdoors.

Despite the lightning, the storm was mild. Only a light mist was falling when a servant directed her to the gardens behind the house. She let her skirt drag in the wet grass, lifting her face to the sky. It felt good to be outside after two entire days in the carriage with her parents. If she could have managed it, Cleo would have hired her own carriage just for herself and Helen, leaving the elder Greys to congratulate themselves on Helen's triumph all the way to Dorset. Their mother, of course, had wanted Helen nearby in case a spasm of delight overcame her again and she needed to smother her daughter in an embrace. Their father hadn't trusted Cleo not to put "radical and absurd" ideas into Helen's head. He'd watched her warily the entire trip, and Cleo had nearly bitten her tongue off a dozen times keeping her silence. And his final warning, delivered even as they drove up the sweeping drive of Kingstag, had almost been too much. She'd had to sit in the carriage a minute and compose herself before getting out.

But she *would* keep her composure, come what may. It was only for a fortnight, and it was for Helen and her wedding. She was aware that her parents had invited her only because Helen wanted her to come. Her father might be ashamed of her and her mother might think her unnatural, but her sister still loved her, and she wouldn't repay that by causing strife and discord.

She slowed down as she reached the gravel paths of the

garden. The Duke of Wessex, no matter that he might be remote and cool when it came to courting a wife, had a lovely garden. She stopped to examine all the plants, marveling at the profusion of greenery and blooms. How on earth did they get them to grow so thickly? Her own house had only a small garden, and nothing seemed to thrive. But these roses! They were everywhere, lush globes of pink and yellow petals that smelled divine. Cleo stuck her face into the flowery bower and sniffed, in paradise. What she wouldn't give for her garden to look like this . . .

And this would be her sister's home. She touched another fragrant rose, spilling a cascade of raindrops onto her skirt. The Duke of Wessex wasn't at all what she had expected. From Helen's description of him, she'd imagined an older man, very elegant and urbane. The man she'd met today was far more masculine. Thick waves of dark hair threatened to tumble over his high forehead, which gave him a somewhat wild look that was at odds with his surprisingly sensual mouth. He was undeniably handsome, but there was an implacable strength in his face as well. Cleo fancied he was a man of strong passions and great control, the sort of man who wouldn't be denied anything he set his heart on.

Then she shook her head at how ridiculous she was, imputing an entire personality to a man she'd only just met. No doubt he'd turn out to be much as Helen described him, once she got to know him a little better. Dukes were far out of her ordinary acquaintance.

She bent down to sniff a peony, trying to squash the seed of worry that had sprouted when Helen confessed to nerves. Her sister was gentle and kind-hearted, and Cleo wasn't at all certain Helen would be able to stand up to a man as intimidating as the duke.

It worried her that Wessex had only called on Helen a few times. How could one marry on such short acquaintance? She could forgive her sister, who had, no doubt, been dazzled by his rank and broad shoulders and very handsome face, but she hoped the duke hadn't chosen Helen because she was beautiful, demure, and dutiful. He must be a very busy man, and if he didn't spend time with his bride, he would never know how wonderful Helen was. And if he made Helen miserable . . .

She sighed and walked on toward the irises. As strong as her instinct was to protect Helen, this was not her battle. Helen had chosen him, and she must have had her reasons. Again her father's warning echoed in her mind: *Hold your tongue or you will be dead to all of us.*

The rain grew a little harder, and she shook out her shawl, intending to drape it over her head. She had two weeks to take the duke's measure. The duke had two weeks to recognize what a jewel Helen was.

"Are you well?"

She jumped at the sound of the voice, dropping her shawl in the process. The man she had just been thinking of stood behind her. "No, no," she said, flustered, then corrected herself. "That is, I'm quite well, thank you. I was just admiring the roses."

The Duke of Wessex stooped to retrieve her shawl. "My mother is a passionate gardener. She'll be pleased you admire her work."

"Very much so," she said with enthusiasm. "They're superb!"

"She does dote upon them," he agreed.

"Everything beautiful must be nurtured and loved." Cleo reached toward a pink rose that climbed up a nearby wall. "Nothing could bloom this profusely without a great deal of care."

He cleared his throat. "And a large contingent of gardeners."

She laughed. "I am sure they help as well, but this is a garden of love. Don't you agree?"

The duke didn't move. "Love?"

Cleo vaguely knew she ought to mention her sister, but the intensity in his dark eyes jangled her thoughts. "Yes. Love for the plants . . . although also a place where one might be moved to steal a kiss in the shrubbery."

She had shocked him. His eyes darkened, and he opened his mouth to speak only to close it again. Oh dear; she'd let her mouth run away from her already.

"Indeed. You may be correct," said the duke before she could apologize. "Forgive me if I interrupted your study of the roses and the—er—shrubbery. I was on my way to see a tree."

"A tree?" she echoed, grasping at a new topic gratefully.

"It was struck by lightning, or so I was told."

Cleo remembered the tremendous crack of lightning when they first arrived. "Oh, yes! I almost fell off the carriage step, it startled me so. I hope the tree didn't damage anything."

His expression was as calm as ever, but his eyes were piercing as he looked at her. "Likely not. We are positively overrun with oaks at Kingstag. I expect we'll all be glad of the lightning when the tree is fueling our fires."

She grinned in surprise, not having expected a duke to pay attention to what went into his fireplaces. "How very practical."

For a moment his gaze seemed to snag on her smile. Cleo wiped it away at once. Oh dear, had her impulsive nature already managed to offend? But all he said was, "Quite."

She wet her lips. The rain was growing harder now, although the duke didn't seem to mind. "I think I ought to go back to the house now. The rain . . ." She held up one hand as if to catch the drops falling around them.

He looked up as if just noticing the rain. "Of course. And here I am, holding your shawl." He handed it back to her.

"Thank you, Your Grace. Until dinner?"

He thrust one hand through his hair, sweeping the wild

locks back over his forehead. It exposed his sharp cheekbones and firm jaw more starkly. Cleo was impressed in spite of herself. Gracious, how could Helen *not* want him to whisk her into the shrubbery? "Until dinner, Mrs. Barrows." He bowed and walked on, his boots crunching on the gravel.

Cleo flung the tail of her shawl over her head and hurried toward the house. Suddenly, two weeks didn't seem so long after all.

$\mathscr{H}$ 3 $\mathscr{K}$

I t was an eternity before the dinner hour finally arrived.

Gareth delayed going to the drawing room. He smoothed his cravat and tugged at his jacket, trying not to notice how his heart seemed to be thudding very hard against his ribs. He hadn't seen his bride since the Greys arrived. That was perfectly expected; no doubt she had wanted a chance to rest from the journey and refresh herself. The fact that he kept picturing Mrs. Barrows—instead of Miss Grey, his chosen bride—reclining against the pillows of her bed was surely just a result of the lightning strike. It must have been closer than he'd thought and disordered his brain. No doubt as soon as he saw her at dinner, he would realize how mistaken that first electrifying impression had been.

Of course, he'd met her for a moment in the garden and nothing had happened to change it. On the contrary; she'd called it a garden of love and mentioned kissing in the shrubbery, and his mind had almost ceased working.

But now it was time to see her, along with his bride and her parents and even—God help him—all his family. His sisters were wildly excited to meet Miss Grey, and his mother had deemed dinner the proper time. Perhaps some of his bride's quiet self-possession would wear off on Bridget especially, he thought, trying not to think how Mrs. Barrows's lively nature was far more like his siblings'.

He took a deep breath. What was the matter with him? It *must* have been the lightning. Once he met the lady in proper, dignified circumstances, he would revert to his usual sane, rational self. Surely a longer acquaintance would confirm what he truly believed, that Helen Grey was the best possible choice for his duchess. She would be an excellent hostess, a kind mother, and a good role model for his sisters. She would look beautiful on his arm. He would have her dowry property, which he had long coveted. Just thinking through the logical, sane reasons why he wanted this match had a calming effect. He had made the right choice, and his odd fascination with her sister was merely a passing flight of fancy.

The door opened behind him and James Blair came in. The storm had blown away, and Blair's expression was once more calm and equable. He would be at dinner tonight as well, as he often was at family dinners or when there was an unescorted lady present. Gareth had even excused him from most of his duties for the next fortnight; Blair had spent a great deal of time around the Greys this spring, and he could help smooth any awkward moments that might arrive as the families mingled. "Ah, there you are. I was beginning to fear you'd left me to face the ladies all by myself."

"Sir William would be there."

"I had hoped for more," said Gareth dryly.

"And here I am." Blair made a grimace. "In desperate need of a drink, I'm afraid."

"Yes." Gareth seized on the word. Now that his cousin mentioned it, a drink sounded like just the thing. "A brilliant idea." He went to the cabinet in the corner and poured two measures of brandy, glad of something to do.

"I've decided to grant your wish regarding Mrs. Barrows," said Blair then, with no warning at all.

The brandy bottle seemed to lurch in his hand, spilling liquor on the silver tray beneath the glass. "What do you mean?" he asked, keeping his back to his cousin as he hastily mopped up the liquid.

"That I act as her escort this fortnight."

"Ah yes." Gareth had forgotten that request. It had seemed a natural one to make a week ago, when all he knew was that Helen Grey's older widowed sister would be part of the party. Blair had already agreed to do that; why did he have to bring it up now? "I thought we'd settled that a week ago."

"I was uncertain." Blair accepted a glass of brandy. "But after meeting her today, I believe I may enjoy her company a great deal."

Gareth was struck motionless. "Why?" was all he managed to ask. Had Blair also met her in the garden? Hadn't he been cowed by the threat of lightning? For some reason, Gareth was wildly irked that his cousin might have seen her with raindrops glistening on her skin. Damn it, maybe they'd better go in to dinner at once, so he could take another long look at her and cure his irrational interest right away.

Blair seemed not to notice his tension. "I suspect she is the source of some tension in the family. There was something about the way she pressed her lips together when she stepped out of the carriage."

He pictured her mouth and took a gulp of his drink. "She's a widow with her own home. Perhaps there's something in her own life, and not her family's, that gave her pause."

"No doubt. She married a shopkeeper when she was only seventeen, and she still owns and runs the shop."

A shopkeeper's wife. Gareth either hadn't paid attention to that part of James's report on the Grey family or hadn't cared enough to remember. "Where is the shop?" he asked, instantly chagrined that he had done so. Why did that matter?

"In Melchester, near Grey's property. A rather large draper's shop."

A draper's shop. He pictured her running her fingers over bolts of brilliant silks, gauzy laces, satin ribbons. He tossed back the last of his brandy. Why did she run the shop? Ladies did no such thing; his mother would have fainted away at the thought of managing a shop. "How independent. What do you suspect, Blair?" He tried to get back to the main topic, which was . . . oh yes. Mrs. Barrows's secrets. The way she pressed her lips together. "Is this shop a dark family secret?"

Blair shook his head. "No, although you won't hear a word about it from Sir William. The man has a supremely inflated sense of himself, and I doubt he approves."

"No, I expect not." Gareth's one overriding impression of his soon-to-be in-laws was pride. Sir William clung to it, and Lady Grey couldn't hide her delight in having a connection to Wessex. He rather doubted a merchant in the family had been as agreeable to the Greys. "Why did she marry a shopkeeper?" he murmured, almost to himself.

"Apparently she loved him." Blair's faint grin returned. "I told you: impulsive, bold, and passionate. She's a woman who isn't afraid to pursue what she wants."

Oh, Lord. He raised his glass and realized it was already empty. "Do you think that might be causing this tension you noticed?" he asked, grasping at Blair's earlier comment.

"I'm not certain." Blair spoke slowly. "Didn't you remark it? I wasn't aware of it earlier, in London, but it was almost palpable when they arrived."

Gareth frowned. He hadn't noticed anything amiss—well, he hadn't noticed much of anything beyond Mrs. Barrows's mouth and eyes and the way her skirt swayed as she climbed the stairs, none of which had struck him as remotely amiss. "I wonder why. Could it be the wedding?" He lowered his voice, watching his cousin closely. "Do you think Miss Grey or her parents want to break the engagement?"

Blair seemed startled. He turned to Gareth, a frown creasing his forehead. "I highly doubt it, Wessex. What made you say that?"

Yes, what *had* made him say that? He had no idea. This morning he had been highly pleased with his impending marriage and his choice of bride. Not one wisp of hesitation had clouded his mind, not even his mother's gentle chiding about love and affection. Then a woman—the wrong woman —looked up at him with sparkling brown eyes and it seemed as though all his logical decisions had been made hastily and foolishly, based on air. Now he had just asked, without any forethought at all, if his bride might be planning to jilt him. Even worse, there had been a thread of hope in his question.

What was wrong with him tonight? His mother had planned a wedding celebration that would be spoken of for years to come. Dozens of guests would be arriving in a matter of days. The marriage contract was signed. The bride was upstairs, probably already planning how she would redecorate when the duchess's suite was hers. The marriage was going to happen. Gareth must have lost his mind to contemplate—let alone contemplate with equanimity—anything else.

"Nothing," he said, telling himself it was true. "You made it sound very ominous, and that was the most alarming thing I could think of on the spot. The wedding is in a fortnight, after all."

Blair's shoulders eased. "Of course."

He cleared his throat. "Yes. Right. Well, thank you for sharing your concern with me. If anything particular comes up, do let me know."

"Of course I will. I shall do my best to learn Mrs. Barrows's secrets."

For some reason, that didn't sit too well with Gareth. He

cast a longing glance at the brandy decanter but resolutely set down his glass. "Shall we go to dinner?"

"Indeed," murmured Blair. "Time to face the enemy."

That fit a little too well with Gareth's own feeling, so he said nothing. They went to the drawing room, where much of the family had already gathered. His sisters had clustered around Miss Grey, chattering with various degrees of animation. Serena and Alexandra, he was pleased to see, were achieving some level of decorum, but Bridget, as feared, was louder and more boisterous than ever. For her part, Miss Grey seemed a little cowed by them. Her smile was uncertain, and she wasn't saying much, although in fairness, it must have been rather intimidating to have three girls discussing every detail of her dress and pelting her with queries about London.

His mother was conversing with Sir William and Lady Grey, who looked up with twin expressions of rapture at his entrance. Gareth joined them as Blair headed for the younger ladies. He had a way with Bridget, and Gareth hoped Blair could calm his sister down so she wouldn't frighten poor Miss Grey to death.

"Good evening, Your Grace, good evening!" Sir William almost preened in his satisfaction. "Delightful house."

"Oh yes," gushed his wife. "I've never seen one finer!"

"How very good of you to say so." He inclined his head, keeping one eye on the door. A quick survey of the room had revealed the absence of Mrs. Barrows.

"If you'll pardon me, I shall have a word with the butler about dinner." His mother lowered her voice as she passed him. "Sophronia has deigned to join us this evening."

"Has she?" Gareth shot her a look. "How generous of her."

"Don't start," she murmured, edging past him. "I tried to dissuade her."

Everyone knew that was hopeless. Nothing dissuaded Sophronia once she set her mind on something. Still, it gave him something to think about as Lady Grey's effusions of delight over Kingstag Castle continued. Everything was perfection, in her opinion, and she seemed determined to list each point. It grew to be a bit much, to tell the truth. Gareth appreciated his home and was pleased to hear it admired, but she went on and on as though praising a gift he had given her. As soon as he could, he excused himself and went to Miss Grey, who appeared more at ease now. Blair had channeled the discussion into the diversions planned for the next fortnight.

"Good evening, Miss Grey." He bowed, and she curtseyed. Very proper. Very reserved. "How have you found Kingstag Castle thus far?"

She smiled. "It is lovely, sir. I look forward to seeing the grounds. Your sisters have described them so well."

"We're going to take her around to see everything!" put in Bridget, beaming. "The lake, the grotto, everything! Only, she doesn't ride terribly well, so James will have to drive us in the barouche."

"I never promised," Blair said with a smile.

"But near enough! I shall be on my best behavior. Please?" she begged.

"Perhaps Wessex will want to show Miss Grey the grounds himself," replied Blair with a glance at Gareth.

"If she wishes," he said. "We shall ride out to see as much as you care to see, Miss Grey."

She lowered her eyes and curtseyed again. "That is very kind of you, sir."

Blair drew the younger girls aside, saying he had an idea for an entertainment later, and they retreated to a corner of the room, although the giggles and whispers were audible to all. Gareth looked at his bride-to-be, and she looked at him. He suddenly realized he had no idea what to say to her, and from the expression on her face, she probably felt the same.

"Your sisters are charming," said Miss Grey.

"They are indeed—and they have been positively wild to make your acquaintance." He watched Alexandra whisper something in Serena's ear, and a slight smile curved his lips at the delight in Bridget's face over whatever they were plotting. His sisters were exhausting, but he did love them. "I hope they haven't been impertinent."

"Not at all." Miss Grey paused. "Sisters are important. I shall be glad to have some more."

"I shall be glad to share them." Gareth repressed the urge to glance at the door yet again at the mention of her sister. He must not allow himself to think what was teasing the edges of his mind. If their conversations were always rather dull, it must be his fault and not hers. When they were better acquainted, they would know what to talk about and not end up in these awkward silences.

"Good evening," said a bright voice behind him. He turned, tamping down the quick spurt of anticipation. This time he was prepared. This time she wouldn't catch him off guard, the earth would remain firmly and motionlessly lodged beneath his feet, and he wouldn't feel as though he'd been hit over the head by a falling tree branch.

Instead he felt as though the breath had been sucked right out of his lungs. Mrs. Barrows wore a gauzy white dress that swirled and clung to her body with every step. A long, narrow shawl of vivid blue looped around her bare arms. Ropes of delicate gold chain looped around her bodice, jingling with little gold coins. Her sable hair was twisted up on her head, more gold chain running through it, and on her feet—her bare feet—were dainty leather sandals. She looked like a Roman goddess, he thought numbly: Venus, the goddess of desire.

"Oh, Cleo, how lovely you look," said Miss Grey warmly.

"Thank you, Helen. The minute the chain came into the shop, I thought to wear it." Mrs. Barrows beamed at her sister as she joined them. "Although I don't think I can compare to you!"

Gareth turned his head to look at his fiancé. He hadn't even noticed what she was wearing. A pale pink dress, very fashionable and very ordinary. His feet had never left the ground once while looking at her.

"Good evening, Your Grace." Mrs. Barrows dipped a curtsey. The little coins tinkled softly as she moved.

"Good evening." His tongue had trouble forming the words.

"Mrs. Barrows." Blair appeared at her elbow with a pleased smile. "Good evening. What an original gown."

She smiled. "Very unoriginal, you mean! I fell in love with an illustration in one of my father's books and longed to recreate it for myself. This design must be two thousand years old."

"But surely even better now," he replied. Blair was looking at her with far too much appreciation, thought Gareth testily. "Don't you agree, Wessex?"

"Er— Yes," he said. At least the question gave him an excuse for staring at her.

She looked directly at him then, her dark eyes sparkling. A little smile curved her mouth into a perfectly kissable shape. Gareth felt a cold sweat break out on the back of his neck. He might need another brandy. "Thank you, Your Grace. You flatter me."

The door opened, and Gareth's mother returned, thank God—although with Sophronia and Henrietta Black in her wake. Sophronia looked as eccentric as ever tonight, in a gown thirty years out of date and her henna-colored hair tied up in a bewildering assortment of braids and knots, but her gaze was as keen and ruthless as ever. Unconsciously Gareth braced himself, sensing that she had decided to join them in order to stir up trouble in some way.

"Isn't it time to eat?" she asked loudly, confirming his

suspicions. Her companion, Henrietta, tried to murmur something in her ear, but Sophronia waved her away. "I'm half-starved after the long walk down here."

"Nearly," said the duchess calmly, guiding her across the room. "Come meet our guests. Here are Sir William and Lady Grey. Wessex is to marry their daughter. Sir William, Lady Grey, may I present you to Lady Sophronia Cavendish?"

"A great honor, madam." Sir William bowed.

"Oh yes, indeed!" trilled his wife, fluttering her hands as though she couldn't contain herself. "A singular pleasure, my lady!"

Sophronia gave the woman a hard stare, then turned away. The duchess quickly intervened. "You must meet the bride!" She gave Gareth a look as Sophronia tottered toward him, and he made the introductions.

Sophronia baldly looked Miss Grey up and down, then did the same to Mrs. Barrows. "Are you the bride?"

Mrs. Barrows blinked. "No, my sister has that happy honor."

The older woman grunted. "She doesn't look honored."

"Sophronia," murmured the duchess in a warning way.

"Oh, but she is!" put in Lady Grey. "Who would not be honored to become the Duchess of Wessex, mistress of Kingstag Castle? I assure you, madam, my daughter feels her honor very, very well!"

"She doesn't show it." The elderly lady's keen eye landed on Mrs. Barrows again. "Already married, are you?"

"No, my lady. I'm a widow." Mrs. Barrows seemed amused by Sophronia. She shot her sister a glance full of impudent amusement. Her mouth twitched as if to keep from laughing. Gareth wondered what her laugh sounded like. What her lips felt like. What she wore underneath that slip of a gown.

God help him.

"You don't dress like one," remarked Sophronia. Once

again she was coming perilously close to rudeness, and as usual, no one seemed to know quite how to deflect her. She peered closer at Mrs. Barrows's gown. "Where did you get that chain? It's quite unusual."

"Oh my heavens!" burst out Lady Grey. Everyone looked at her and her face seemed to fill with panic for a moment. "I —I beg your pardon, Your Grace, I have just remembered something I must tell my daughter."

"Yes, Mama," murmured Miss Grey, stepping forward.

"No, Helen dear." Her mother's voice was high and strained. "Your sister."

Miss Grey's eyes flickered to Mrs. Barrows's. Something passed between them, but Gareth wasn't sure what. Suddenly he understood what Blair had meant about a tension in the Grey family. Even Mrs. Barrows's supple mouth looked flat. "We're about to go in to dinner, Mama," she said, her voice quiet and reserved. There was none of the warmth and humor she had shown before.

Lady Grey's face pinched. "It will only take a moment, Cleo. Come here."

"Well, Alice, is it time to eat or isn't it? I never had the patience to stand around waiting for my dinner." Sophronia turned to the duchess, who began to look a little strained as well.

"Yes, dinner is ready." The duchess nodded at one of the footmen, who swept open the doors.

"Thank goodness," declared Bridget, bounding across the room. Alexandra and Serena followed more sedately. "I'm so hungry!"

"That's my girl," said Sophronia with approval as the duchess closed her eyes in despair. "Who's going to escort me? I see you haven't got nearly enough gentlemen tonight, Wessex."

"The guests will begin arriving tomorrow," he replied.

"Blair will give you his arm tonight." He nodded at his cousin.

Sophronia grunted. "I suppose he'll do." She put out her hand, and Blair obediently gave her his arm.

The duchess smiled at the rest of them. "Since we are just family tonight, I thought we could all go in together. I hope you will forgive the informality."

There was a murmur of assent. Gareth turned to Lady Grey, still hovering behind him. What the devil had she wanted to tell Mrs. Barrows so urgently? And why had it banished the light from the lady's eyes? Even now, she was staring fixedly at the carpet, her lower lip caught between her teeth. He felt again the oddest sensation of falling. He wanted to shake her mother—her own mother—for dampening her spirits. He must be going mad. "May I escort you, madam?"

Lady Grey hesitated, but after exchanging a glance with her husband, she took Gareth's arm. "Why yes, how kind, Your Grace! I have heard such reports of your chef at Kingstag, I expect dinner shall be utterly incomparable . . ." She went on, but he barely heard her. His sisters fell in step with Miss Grey behind them, and they followed his mother into the dining room.

But when he reached the dining room and seated Lady Grey, he discovered that Mrs. Barrows and Sir William had not followed them.

4

"Stay a moment," growled Sir William at his older daughter as the others left the room. Cleo waited, burning with humiliation. The momentary relief she'd felt when the Duke of Wessex intercepted her mother had quickly been replaced by dread when her father gave her a black look behind the duke's back. For a moment there, she'd been blessing the duke with all her might, but of course the coming confrontation couldn't be avoided.

Her father waited until everyone else had left, then stared fiercely at the footman until the servant closed the door, leaving them in complete privacy. Even then, he spoke in a harsh whisper. "You think very highly of yourself, don't you? When will you cease trying to humiliate us at every turn by bringing up your wretched little trade?"

"It is not wretched," she said quietly.

He snorted. "It is indeed! My own daughter, laboring in a shop like some baseborn chit. It is intolerable, I tell you, *intolerable*. The very least you could do is remember your place here and kindly keep your idle thoughts and opinions to yourself."

"What is my place?" she asked before she could stop

herself. Perhaps he wouldn't be able to tell her. Perhaps he had some trace of affection left for her.

"A tradesman's widow," he said with a snort. "Utterly beneath your ancestors! Your sister will be a duchess, and you stand in her drawing room and loudly proclaim yourself little better than a common servant!" Cleo's mouth opened in shock, and he went on. "Sometimes I wonder precisely who you think you are, miss!"

"You named me for a queen," she said. "Who do you think I am?"

He harrumphed. "What a laughable mistake. Cleopatra was born to royalty and she knew her place. Don't think so highly of yourself, miss."

"But she led her country," Cleo reminded him. "I daresay someone thought that wasn't her place."

Her father glowered at her. "She did not go against her parents' wishes and lower herself to go into trade."

"She lowered herself to marrying her brother," Cleo murmured. "Although I suppose that was at her parents' wish."

He closed his eyes and exhaled, then shot her another sharp glance. "You've done as you wished, and I have not disowned you. But don't think I'm proud of your actions. You're only welcome here because your sister wished it. It is her wedding—she, at least, will take her proper place in society, while you have done precious little for our family."

Cleo shifted her weight back and forth, setting her skirt to swirling about her ankles. The tiny coins clinked softly. "I paid for Helen's wardrobe."

"Shh!" hissed her father, glancing around anxiously, as though the duke might hear her words all the way in the dining room. "Don't tell everyone!" He gave a snort. "Bad enough that my daughter has to operate a shop like a common merchant. You'd tell the world I must accept your charity, too."

"It's not charity," she protested. "I wanted to help! Helen is my sister."

"Then mind your tongue," he snapped. "Do you want to embarrass her in front of her future husband? Do you want him to think us a pack of penniless, hysterical fools?"

Cleo watched the coins settle into silence again. "No, Papa. I'm sorry."

"You should be." With that, he brushed past her, only waiting at the door to offer his arm. As angry as he was with everything she did, he would never break protocol and leave her to walk into the dining room alone. *We must keep up appearances, after all,* Cleo thought, pasting a wooden smile on her face, feeling oddly detached from her father even as her hand rested on his arm.

She knew her parents hadn't understood when she and Matthew eloped; she hadn't expected them to. The years of her marriage had been rather cool ones between her and her parents, but still civil. Cleo knew why; her mother had once outright admitted that if she had to be the wife of a shopkeeper, at least she was the wife of a very prosperous shopkeeper. At the time, she'd wondered who her parents thought she would marry. The Greys had had no money for as long as she could remember, and no connections of consequence. Suitors had been rare in their house.

But whatever their initial hopes for her, it was clear that all the burden of making a great match had descended upon Helen. Cleo felt sorry for that. She had been so happy with Matthew and wished the same for her sister, whether it was with a duke or a lowly tailor. She got some glimpse of what her sister must have endured after Matthew died. Her father had tried to insist that she sell her shop and return home. Unspoken was the presumption that she would make a better match the second time, now that she was a widow of some modest fortune. After that conversation, Cleo had made only the briefest visits home. She had no desire to settle into a ladylike uselessness in her widowhood. Working in the shop reminded her of Matthew, and Cleo liked being responsible for herself. She could support herself, it turned out, so why shouldn't she? Without the shop, she would have precious little of her own: no children, no husband, no income . . . nothing to keep her mind occupied. What else was she to do with herself?

The unfairness of her father's feelings made her want to scream. Never mind that her shop, which he hated, supplied her money, which he somehow managed to accept. At times she had been almost determined to stop offering it, since the source of the income was so hateful to both her parents. Perhaps they would be more appreciative if they felt the lack of her "common merchant" funds. But cutting them off would mean cutting off Helen as well. Helen was the dearest person in the world to her; Helen had wished her joy when she married Matthew. And now she had made a splendid match to the illustrious Duke of Wessex—even if he did seem awfully reticent and reserved—and Cleo would never regret helping her sister find happiness.

That was the thought she must keep in the forefront of her mind for the next few weeks. Stirring up an argument with either one of her parents would only cause Helen anxiety, and she had absolutely no wish to embarrass her sister in front of the Cavendish family.

5

T he guests began to arrive the next day. The house came alive with trills of female voices, and the jangle of harnesses was almost constant. Cleo had marveled at the size of the castle when they arrived, but after a while she began to wonder where all these guests would stay. Surely even Kingstag Castle couldn't hold them all.

Helen, of course, had to greet everyone, welcoming them at the duchess's side. Cleo joined her, losing herself in the excitement of meeting new people, none of whom seemed to recoil at the sight of her, common merchant though she was. Perhaps that was because she said nothing at all about herself, speaking only of her sister and the wedding and how lovely the castle was.

"I'm starting to sound like Mama," she whispered to her sister after a while. "All I can speak of is Kingstag!"

Helen sighed. "There is a great deal to say about it."

"Well, it truly is magnificent." Cleo craned her neck to admire the vaulted ceiling of the hall, which put her in mind of a cathedral. The house was full of modern improvements— there was indeed piping for water inside the house—but it retained much of its ancient air as well. "To think, you'll be mistress of this in a few days! Do you remember when we used to dream of living in a castle?"

Her sister smiled. "Yes. But even then I never dreamt of one this enormous."

"All the more to explore!" Cleo grinned, but finally realized how pale her sister had become. "Helen, are you well?" she asked in concern. "You should sit down."

There was a distant rattle of wheels on gravel. Helen turned toward the open door. "I can't. Someone else is arriving."

"Let Her Grace greet them. Come," she urged. "I'm sure the duke wouldn't want his guests to first see you passed out on the floor."

"No, indeed," said a male voice behind them.

Cleo jerked around. The Duke of Wessex stood there, watching in his intent way. His wasn't a merry, fond countenance, but she had the feeling that he paid closer attention than most people. Even in this trifling circumstance, she felt the force of his regard in every fiber of her being. No wonder he was such a powerful man. She could barely drag her eyes away from his.

"Your Grace." Helen dipped a graceful curtsey. "We did not expect you."

"I had some pressing business to attend to this morning; my apologies." He barely glanced at her. "What makes you think your sister is about to faint, Mrs. Barrows?"

Cleo wet her lips and darted a wary glance at her sister. Helen might have been a statue, from all the emotion or energy she conveyed. "She looks pale to me, Your Grace, but perhaps I'm imagining things."

"I would never discount the keen eye of a loving sister." He turned the blast of his regard upon Helen, who seemed to waver on her feet under it. "I agree with Mrs. Barrows, my dear. You must sit down."

"As you wish, Your Grace."

Cleo rolled her eyes. Now that the mighty Wessex had given his approval, Helen would sit. Still, she wasn't one to cast aside help, so she merely took her sister's arm and helped her into the nearby morning parlor, where a pair of elegant settees stood in front of the windows. Helen sank onto one, and Cleo perched on the edge of the facing settee. In the bright sunlight, her sister's face looked drawn and lined, as if she had aged since they arrived. It was distinctly odd, and Cleo frowned in worry. Her sister should be glowing with happiness, or at least contentment. Instead she looked like she had come down with some wasting disease.

Wessex followed. He rang the servants' bell, then closed the door. He came and seated himself next to Cleo, opposite his bride. "Why are you unwell, my dear?"

"I'm only a little tired, Your Grace," said Helen. "A few moments' rest, and I shall return to greeting guests with Her Grace, your mother."

"Nonsense," said Cleo. "You need to eat something; you hardly ate a bite of breakfast. There is no color in your cheeks at all."

Wessex glanced at her. "Is this true, Miss Grey? Was breakfast not to your liking?"

Helen's eyes widened in alarm. "Oh, it was delicious, Your Grace—I simply couldn't choose . . ."

"Perhaps a tot of brandy will restore you," he suggested.

Without thinking, Cleo snorted. "Don't be ridiculous! She's hardly eaten. Brandy will make her faint dead away."

Slowly he turned to her. "What?"

"Tea would be better. Tea and some muffins. Ladies don't normally drink brandy, sir."

"I see," he murmured, still watching her. "A pity, that."

Yes, it was a pity, in Cleo's opinion. She liked a little nip of brandy now and then—never enough to make her head spin, just a small amount after dinner in the winter or perhaps a drop in her tea on especially trying days. Still, her mother would have an apoplexy if she admitted that to the duke, so she merely smiled. "I think the muffins are particularly important. There were some delicious ones at breakfast this morning. May I send for some for my sister?"

"Of course." As if on cue, a servant slipped into the room. Wessex arched one brow at Cleo. "What shall we send for?"

"Tea, please, with milk and muffins. And if there is any of that superb gooseberry jam, that would be lovely." Cleo smiled at the servant, who bowed and hurried off. "Are the guests to arrive all day, Your Grace?"

"I've no idea," he said without a trace of concern. "My mother will know, but she's also quite capable of greeting them herself. I believe the first arrivals were to be family, in any event."

She had to purse her lips to keep from grinning. "And you've no desire to see your family?"

"They will be here for a fortnight at the least." He sounded resigned. "I will see them quite enough."

"Perhaps some of the other guests will prove more diverting." She couldn't resist a naughty smile at his measuring look. "What are guests for, if not to provide entertainment?"

For the first time, his mouth curved. With his head tipped thoughtfully to one side, and that slow, slight grin, he looked sly and devastatingly attractive. "I devoutly hope you are correct."

"I have great expectations," she told him. "Your cousin in particular has promise."

"Ah—you must mean Jack." The duke's grin grew wider. "I believe he inspired a formulation of smelling salts. I would suggest that you tease him about it, but he cannot be teased; on the contrary, he is quite proud of it."

"Yes, *very* promising," repeated Cleo with enthusiasm. "Dare I ask what he did to inspire smelling salts?"

"I don't recall all the details." The duke made a bored grimace even though his eyes shone with amusement. "It began with a wager, naturally, and took place during one of the most elegant balls of the season, but I never knew why there was a bow and arrow involved. And as for the monkey . . . well, the less said about the monkey, the better."

"A real monkey?" she asked, trying not to laugh.

"Pungently real," he confirmed. "Lady Hartington swore it took a month to get the smell out of her house."

Cleo laughed. She had a strong feeling Wessex almost envied his cousin. Goodness, he was far from the stuffy duke she had thought him yesterday. He had a dry wit that charmed her, and he was devilishly appealing when he grinned. "No wonder he's famous!"

"Infamous," said the duke, though that slight grin still curved his mouth. "But even Lady Hartington forgave him. Apparently he has this way of smiling at ladies that makes them forgive and forget, even when he looses a monkey in their homes. It prompted some wit to declare that there ought to be a smelling salt to combat the effects of that smile, and thus a legend was born."

Opposite her, Helen sighed, and she abruptly remembered herself. "Not that I think Lord Willoughby will upset the wedding! Indeed, he had better not, or I shall take measures —and I will neither forgive nor forget," she added with a quick laugh. "Never fear, Helen, nothing shall mar your wedding day."

Her sister smiled wanly, glancing at the duke. "I never thought it would."

"Jack is a bit of a rogue, but he's to stand up with me," Wessex assured them. "I would never have asked him if I couldn't rely on him."

"I would never question your judgment, Your Grace," Helen murmured. "See, Cleo, there is nothing to fear."

The duke's grin faded. "No. Nothing at all."

An awkward silence fell over the room. Cleo looked down at her hands, shaken to realize she really liked Wessex's smile.

Not merely in the manner of a woman gratified to see some warmth and humor in her sister's future husband. No, her thoughts had not touched on Helen at all. For a moment, she had quite forgotten why they were there, and her appreciation had been purely female. Which was wrong in so many ways.

It was a relief when the servant returned with a tray. Cleo busied herself with fixing a cup for Helen, keeping her attention firmly on the tea and her sister. Wessex said nothing, but she could feel him watching her. She steadfastly resisted the urge to watch him back. She had a terrible feeling it would be hard to look away again. After a few moments, the duke wished Helen well again and excused himself. When the door clicked closed behind him, she almost wilted.

"Thank you, Cleo," said Helen before she could speak. "I don't know what I would do without you here."

She smiled uneasily. "Live in less anxiety that I'll offend the duke?"

"He didn't appear offended by anything you said." Helen sipped the tea. Some color was already coming back into her cheeks. "He didn't appear bored, either, as he always does when I speak to him."

"Nonsense!"

"If not bored, then he looks as though his mind is elsewhere."

"You mustn't let him do that . . ."

"How can I stop him?" Helen sighed. "He finds me dull."

Cleo sat in tense silence for a moment. She had a terrible feeling it was the truth. Wessex had barely looked at Helen while he sat with them; he had looked at *her*, and she had liked it. That must be corrected at once. "He had better begin to pay you more attention. Then he'll see how sweet and charming and lovely you are."

"Oh, Cleo." Her sister smiled wistfully. "Not everyone

sees me as you do. I'm not vivacious and capable of speaking to anyone, as you are."

"Which makes you a far better companion, since you never say anything hurtful or rash, as I do."

Helen stared into her tea. "I am sure, after a few years, the duke and I will have learnt how to get on with each other. I will learn what pleases him, and he has already been so solicitous of me. We will learn."

"Er . . . yes." She worked to keep the frown from her face. Every time she talked with her sister, it became less and less clear why Helen had accepted his proposal. Did her sister merely want to be a duchess? Was he simply too eligible, too handsome, too wealthy to refuse? Had Papa forced her to accept? Cleo wasn't sure she even wanted to know if the last was true. Her father would never forgive her if she stirred up trouble, and yet . . . "Are—are you pleased with this marriage, Helen?" Her sister looked up warily. Cleo wet her lips. "I presumed you were, when you accepted His Grace's proposal, but . . . I cannot help but notice how listless you are. It's as if something you dread is approaching, rather than something joyful."

For a long moment Helen said nothing. "My marriage won't be like yours," she finally whispered. "His Grace doesn't love me as Matthew loved you. I don't expect him to —I daresay most men of his rank don't love their wives—and I knew that when I accepted his proposal. I suppose it's just becoming real to me now, that he and I will be married in a few days."

"You don't have to marry him." It popped out of her mouth before Cleo could stop it.

Helen's dark eyes widened in alarm. "Don't say such a thing! Of course I do. The guests are arriving! I couldn't possibly jilt His Grace."

You could if you really didn't want to marry him, thought Cleo. She bit her lip, hard, to keep the thought unspoken.

"It's just nerves," went on Helen, a bit more firmly. She took a sip of tea. "Becoming mistress of this house, part of this family, a duchess . . . It's very overwhelming, but I shall do my best. Please don't tell Papa anything."

"No," Cleo said after a pause. "I wouldn't." She hardly wanted to speak to her father at all, especially with this new suspicion in her mind that he had browbeaten Helen into accepting Wessex. She took a deep breath and shook off her worries. Perhaps it was just bridal nerves. Helen was reserved, but she was no shrinking violet. She would find her way; the Cavendish family was warm and welcoming, and he wasn't unkind or cold at all. Cleo thought it would be very easy to fall in love with the duke. And surely once Wessex spent more time with Helen, he would see what a lovely person she was and fall deeply in love with her. It was impossible not to love Helen, once one knew her.

And if an opportunity presented itself to nudge His Grace a little closer to that happy state, Cleo would be prepared to take it.

GARETH LEFT THE HOUSE, AVOIDING THE FRONT OF THE CASTLE where yet another carriage was arriving. His mother had planned the wedding and guest list, and as far as he was concerned, she could welcome every distant cousin and acquaintance who came. Normally he would be busy as usual, off in his study or out riding the estate. If he had any discipline, he'd return to his study now. Or more accurately, if he had any discipline, he never would have left it and gone down to the hall where he knew his bride and her sister were greeting guests. He knew because Blair had mentioned it as they sat down to work. And if his cousin had deliberately set out to destroy Gareth's peace of mind, he couldn't have done a better job. Within an hour Gareth had admitted defeat and gone to see for himself.

He didn't want to think about why.

The contrast between the two sisters couldn't have been sharper. Helen, his future wife, held herself with perfect poise, her hands clasped in front of her. Her smile was polite, her manner reserved. She was lovely, from the top of her glossy dark curls to the tips of her pink slippers peeking out from beneath her snow-white skirts. She was every inch the perfect duchess.

Mrs. Barrows, on the other hand, was like a bolt of light in the dark expanse of the hall. Her dress was blue, with bold embroidery on the skirt and—God help him for noticing—all over the bodice. Her smile was wide and warm. She greeted the arriving guests as though she were truly delighted to meet them, her hands as animated as her face. He lurked at the back of the hall and watched her laugh with his cousin Jack Willoughby, and a tendril of something like jealousy circled his gut.

Speaking to her, though, hadn't helped at all. He'd been spurred forward by an apparent argument between the sisters, and he'd told himself he was being a solicitous fiancé, urging his bride to sit down and rest, as she did look rather pale. But then her sister spoke to him, and he'd almost forgotten his future wife was in the room.

Cleopatra. She was well named. Gareth could easily see men being willing to fight and die for her. How could two sisters be so unlike? And why, by all that was sane and reasonable, was he so mesmerized by the wrong one?

He had to stop this. He must think of Miss Grey—Helen. Perhaps if he called her by name, he would feel closer to her. Helen, Helen, Helen.

He walked down the gravel path that led to the stables. One of the ancient oaks that grew along the path had been felled, split right to the roots by lightning in the recent storm. It had fallen away from the carriage lane, but it would take weeks to clear the debris. There would be firewood for a year from that tree. Several men were working on it and doffed their caps as he walked by. Gareth nodded at them and walked on.

The Kingstag stables were spacious, laid out with a small courtyard in the center. The stalls could house almost eighty horses at a time, although in recent years they had rarely done so. Since Gareth's father's death, his mother had chosen to remain quietly in the country while raising her young daughters. Now he supposed there would be more entertaining at Kingstag; not only would he have a wife but his sisters would be making their debuts soon, which would necessitate balls and parties and all manner of visitors. He suspected his mother was looking forward to it, given her enthusiasm for the wedding plans. He remembered how much she had loved hosting parties and soirees when he was young. It was the only reason he had agreed to a large wedding celebration. Left to his own devices, he would have been happy to wed in the bishop's private quarters.

He wondered what Helen wanted. He hoped his mother had consulted her.

A shiny black phaeton with startling yellow wheels currently stood in the stable courtyard. Grooms were unhitching a pair of large black stallions, although their actions were slowed by the awestruck glances they kept bestowing on the carriage. It must be Jack's. If it wasn't, Gareth would wager half his estate it *would* be Jack's by the end of the week. His cousin was drawn to beauty like a bee to a flower, and this phaeton cast all others into the shade.

"Did you win it, steal it, or borrow it?" he asked loudly.

Jack Willoughby stepped out from behind his carriage. "I'm wounded. Naturally I bought her. Had to borrow a bit, but she's mine."

"She?"

"Hippolyta." Jack whispered the name with the reverence

of a lover. He reached out and rubbed a spot of dirt from the gleaming wheels. "Hippolyta, my beauty."

"You named your phaeton." Gareth shook his head. "Of course you did."

"Just look at her, Wessex! Such curves, such elegance! Have you ever seen a female finer than this?"

Cleo Barrows's laughing face flashed into his mind. Gareth exhaled. "As a matter of fact, yes."

His cousin grimaced. "You always did do things the right way. Besotted with your bride already!"

He closed his eyes. God, he needed a drink—and it wasn't even noon. "You brought the ring?"

"Of course." Jack had gone back to gazing lovingly at Hippolyta. "Got it from the jeweler yesterday."

For a moment there, he'd been almost hopeful Jack would have forgotten it. Lost it. Wagered it away in a card game. The ring was a family heirloom, sent off to a London jeweler to be sized and cleaned. If Jack had forgotten it . . . But the ring was here, so the wedding wouldn't be delayed by the need to procure another one.

"Excellent," Gareth murmured. "Are you headed up to the house?"

"Not yet." Jack took out his handkerchief and reached up to polish another spot on the carriage. "Too many girls in white dresses, giggling like mad. I may spend the next week here in your stables."

"I'll send Withers out with some port and a blanket."

Jack grinned. "Very sporting of you, Wessex."

Gareth nodded and left. He turned away from the house; if Jack wasn't going back, neither was he. There was nothing at the house but trial and temptation right now, as long as Helen and Cleo would be standing in the hall, the contrast between them sharpened by their proximity.

He had to cure himself of this unwanted fascination. He was the Duke of Wessex. He'd had his pick of women in

England and he'd chosen Helen. He wished he could return to that certainty that she was the one. He wished he could feel any sort of contentment about his rapidly approaching marriage to her. He would even be glad just to be less attracted to Cleo; then he would be able to persuade himself that all would work out right in the end, that he would come to care for Helen, that they would all be happy eventually.

Instead . . . all he felt was dread, growing stronger by the hour.

❧ 6 ❧

When they had been at Kingstag several days, Cleo decided to catch up on her correspondence. She'd been away from her shop for several days now, and although she'd left Mr. Mabry, her most trusted clerk, in charge, there were decisions only she could make. A packet of reports and letters had arrived from Mabry the previous day, and she needed to read them.

Reading them would also, she hoped, restore her sense. A week at Kingstag had been both wonderful and a trial. Wonderful, because it truly was the loveliest estate she'd ever seen, from the sprawling splendor of the house to the grounds that seemed to encompass every beauty to be found in England. The food was superb, the servants were well trained, and even the guests were interesting and pleasant for the most part.

And yet it was a trial, because everywhere she saw the duke. Just a glimpse of him across the dining room was enough to make her heart skip a beat. She told herself it was just the awe of meeting a duke; she'd once been presented to a viscount, but nobility had been rare in her corner of the world before this week.

The correspondence, on the other hand, was her life—bills from the silk warehouses, requests from customers, and overdue accounts. A fortnight at Kingstag was an interlude, not a permanent change. She was very much out of place here and always would be.

She gathered her writing case and letters and set out in search of a quiet spot. It was too beautiful a day to remain indoors, bright and extremely warm. Thinking the lake might offer a secluded spot as well as some breeze, she headed down the shaded path along the side of the back lawn, pausing to marvel at the remains of the giant oak that lay beside the path. The trunk was charred black in places and looked as though it had been ripped from the ground. One of the men working to cut it up told her it had been hit by lightning a few days before. That must be the tree the duke had mentioned going to see when she met him in the garden. She was still shaking her head over it as she passed the path to the stables, when the one man she hoped to avoid stepped out in front of her.

"Good morning, Mrs. Barrows."

Just the sound of his voice made her heart jump. "Good morning," she replied. "I was setting out to explore your magnificent estate a little, if I may."

"You must treat it as your own home." His eye dropped to the writing case she carried. "May I carry that for you?"

Oh dear. Cleo tried to smother the little frisson of anticipation that shot through her veins. He had clearly just come back from riding and was even more appealingly masculine in riding clothes than in his evening wear. "You must have a dozen things to do . . ."

He glanced over his shoulder down the path to the stables, where male voices could dimly be heard shouting "Huzzah!" "On the contrary. I would like nothing better than a bit of a walk. Unless, of course, you preferred to walk alone."

He was her host. It was only polite to accept, which must

explain why she accepted at once. "Not at all! I would be honored." She surrendered the writing case with a smile.

"How have you found Kingstag?" he asked as they strolled along the lane.

"It's magnificent," she said. "My mother hasn't exaggerated in the slightest."

"I'm not certain angels dwell in the attics," he said dryly, "but I'm delighted you've found it comfortable and welcoming."

"Did she really say angels in the attics?" Cleo tried and failed to bite back a laugh. "Well, she's very pleased by it, and the excitement might have gone to her head a little."

"I could seat her next to Sophronia, who would point out every draught and inconvenience of the house."

Cleo shook her head. "It would make no difference. My mother is determined to see no fault, even if the ceiling should collapse before her eyes. She would only exclaim over how rustic it looked to have a pile of rubble in the dining room."

He laughed. "That would be too rustic for me. I prefer solid walls and ceilings."

"As do I. The grounds may actually be perfect, though," she went on, shading her eyes with one hand to survey the lake, sparkling in the distance. Willow fronds waved above their heads, dappling the path with sunlight, and the scent of honeysuckle sweetened the air. "I don't know how anyone even notices the house in these surroundings."

"My mother deserves much of the credit. She created the landscape as much as the gardens." He glanced at her, and Cleo felt her face warm. Not just a garden of love, but a whole landscape. "In fact, I seem to recall a nuncheon for the ladies in the garden today."

She smiled uneasily at the veiled question. Nuncheon in the garden would include her mother. For the first few days, it had been enough for Millicent to bask in her role as mother of the bride, which was trying but not unexpected. Lately, though, Millicent had become almost unbearable in her delight, and when she wasn't praising Kingstag in some way, she was fretting at Cleo about being proper and respectable. In the decade since she'd left home Cleo had got used to her freedom, and her patience for her mother's anxious, inane chatter was wearing thin. And if her mother knew that the Duke of Wessex was carrying the drapery shop correspondence from Mr. Mabry at this moment, she'd probably faint dead away. "I have some letters to write and thought I might get a bit of exercise as well. I miss the outdoors."

The duke nodded. "Your shop, I suppose, keeps you indoors a great deal."

Cleo jerked, glancing at him in alarm. She wasn't to talk about her shop at all, not to anyone, but especially not to him. But he was watching her with those dark, dark eyes, and she felt compelled to answer.

"Yes," she murmured. "It does."

"Mr. Blair tells me it's quite a prosperous business," he went on. Cleo couldn't resist a quick glance over her shoulder, half expecting her mother to be lurking nearby, but they were quite alone. "Quite an achievement."

"Yes, for a woman," she said, too late hearing the edge in her voice. She forced a smile as he looked at her, his eyebrows raised. "My apologies," she said hastily. "I shouldn't have spoken so."

"No," he corrected her. "You should speak as you feel."

Cleo fastened her eyes on the path in front of them and they walked in silence for a few minutes. "I was wrong," she said when her voice was even and calm again. "I shouldn't have spoiled our walk."

"I don't think it's been spoiled at all." He was remarkably unruffled. "It's a draper's shop, I believe?"

"Yes," she said politely. There seemed no reason to lie about it.

"Is it a large one? I have little experience of draper's shops."

Cleo was torn. On one hand, he sounded genuinely interested, and she was proud enough of her business to want to talk about it. On the other hand, her parents would have an apoplexy if they discovered it. "Moderately," she said, erring on the side of modesty.

"And yet you manage it on your own?"

"Does that surprise you?"

He tipped his head in contemplation. "I confess I have no idea what's required to run a draper's shop. I imagine it's a great deal of effort, though. When my sisters descend upon the shop in Dorchester they are gone for hours, and one can only pity the poor proprietor, worn out from being sent back and forth for ribbons and lace and bolts of every sort of fabric sold in England." He grimaced as Cleo almost choked on her laughter.

"It's never that dreadful," she protested. "Many aspects are quite enjoyable. Every year I travel to London to visit the warehouses and order the latest fabrics before anyone else has seen them. Nothing is more satisfying than spotting a beautiful piece of silk and knowing exactly which customer it will suit. My clerks do most of the fetching in the shop, but I quite like helping ladies choose the right colors and trimmings. A fine gown is a significant expense and ought to please the wearer for years to come. Most ladies are very grateful to have another woman's approval before making the purchase. Men should understand; I know perfectly well most of the gentlemen here have spent a great deal of time in the stables admiring a carriage." He gave her a sideways glance, and she grinned. "That, and drinking the many bottles of port I saw a footman carrying to the stables."

Wessex coughed. "And a new gown is like a carriage?"

"To most ladies, a new gown is far, far more important than any carriage," she confirmed.

The duke chuckled. "You have illuminated one of the great mysteries of life. I begin to see why Alexandra was reduced to tears when Bridget mocked her bonnet."

"Well, mocking is never kind. She might have suggested a different ribbon, or less trimming."

"Bridget's way is rarely diplomatic," he said in resignation.

Cleo, who rather liked the impetuous girl, waved one hand. "She has time to learn. I was very like her when I was younger, and we all endure difficult ages only to come out the better for them."

"That is very encouraging," he said. "Bridget is . . . a challenge."

"Lady Alexandra and Lady Serena are very poised young ladies. I'm sure Lady Bridget will grow into it." She paused, remembering the disputes and heartfelt conversations with her own sister when they were girls. Without Helen, she didn't know what she would have done. "They are fortunate to have each other. They seem quite close, your sisters."

"Devilishly." He stopped and turned. "In fact . . . Serena?" he called.

First one girl, then another, and so on until no fewer than five young ladies emerged from behind a nearby hedge, looking guilty. "Yes, Wessex?" asked the eldest, a girl with auburn hair and the same intense dark eyes as the duke.

"You're far from the house," he remarked.

"We're not doing anything wrong," blurted out Bridget Cavendish. "It's that horrid pest Henry—"

"Shh!" hissed Charlotte Ascot—sister to the horrid pest, if Cleo remembered correctly. "I swear he can hear his name from a mile away."

"We're just out for a walk," said Serena with a bright smile. "As are you, I see." She curtseyed to Cleo. "I hope you are enjoying your visit to Kingstag, Mrs. Barrows."

"Very much so," she replied warmly. "I simply had to see more of it and walked out in search of adventure."

"Capital!" declared Bridget with a beaming smile. "Would you like to see the grotto? James was supposed to drive us on a tour but he's disappeared."

"*All* the gentlemen have disappeared," muttered Kate Lacy with a very fetching pout. "They only turn up when there's a cricket match."

"Or a game of battledore," put in Charlotte. "Which is even less entertaining to watch, even if that handsome Mr. Newnham is playing."

"No, I much prefer to watch Lord Everett play cricket," said Miss Lacy with a dreamy look on her face.

"They can't have all disappeared into thin air!" burst out Bridget. "We just have to keep looking—" She froze, looking at her brother in alarm.

Wessex, though, merely grinned. "I can hardly turn traitor on my fellow man, can I?"

"And will you tell Mama?" asked Alexandra cautiously.

"We aren't doing anything wrong!" cried Bridget again. "We're just . . . just—" She glanced at her companions. "Just trying to be good hostesses. What if the gentlemen have disappeared because they're bored to death of Kingstag and need reviving from their stupors?"

The duke glanced at Cleo, mirth glinting in his gaze. "No one accused you of doing wrong. But I doubt you'll need to revive anyone from a stupor—not until the ball, that is."

A chorus of protests went up. "No! The ball is the only worthy event!" "Who could fall into a stupor at a ball?" "The gentlemen wouldn't dare try to miss the ball, would they, Wessex? Mama would be furious!"

The duke held up his hands. "I'm sure they'll all be at the ball. Just as I'm sure you ought not to wander too far away. If Mama misses you, nothing I say will save you. It would be a terrible shame to miss the ball as punishment . . ."

He let his suggestion trail off as the girls stared at him in shocked horror. Without a word they turned toward the house, although as she passed Cleo, Bridget did whisper once more, "You really ought to see the grotto!"

Cleo laughed and waved farewell. For a moment she and the duke stood and watched them go, some with steps dragging and some putting their heads together to whisper.

"So that's why the men have congregated in the stables," she remarked. "Not merely the lure of a top-notch phaeton."

He cleared his throat. "I don't know anything about that."

Cleo laughed again.

"Although . . ." Wessex glanced at his sisters' retreating figures. "One does sympathize."

"Frightened by a group of girls?" she asked mischievously.

A faint smile crossed his face. "When Bridget is one of their number? Yes."

On impulse, she added, "Where is the grotto?"

The duke looked at her, his eyebrows slightly raised. For a moment everything seemed to fade away but the two of them. Cleo felt again the mixture of attraction and alarm that had tugged at her in the parlor the other day. She wet her lips. "That's twice now that Lady Bridget has mentioned it. I've never seen a grotto. Is it very dark and mysterious?"

His gaze dropped to her mouth. "Yes."

Oh no. No, no, no. She held out her hand and forced a shaky smile to her lips. "Excellent! Perhaps I shall visit it some other day, after I've written my letters."

He hesitated, then handed her the writing case. The weight of it seemed to help hold her feet to the ground; she was a lowly merchant, not someone a duke would find fascinating. She would take her bills and inventory reports, and he would go back to his castle. "You might find a quiet spot by the lake. There are blankets in the boathouse."

She nodded. "Thank you."

He looked as though he might say something else, but after a moment he merely bowed. "Good day, Mrs. Barrows." He turned and walked back the way they had come, without looking back.

Cleo knew, because she watched him until he disappeared from sight.

Gareth joined Blair on the way to the bowling green a couple of days later. He hadn't planned to go when his mother told him she had planned a day of bowls, but by now he conceded that he was unable to concentrate as usual. *Besides, it is the proper thing for a host to join his guests*, he told himself as he caught sight of the green, some distance from the house. The ladies reposed under the awnings, enjoying refreshments. A pair of young boys were on the green, arguing over something with fingers pointed and an occasional stamp of a foot. But otherwise there was something decidedly off about the scene.

"Where are the gentlemen?" he asked.

"In the stables."

"All of them?" exclaimed Gareth.

Blair grinned. "Willoughby's refuge has proven enormously popular."

"That damned phaeton." Gareth shook his head. He knew several men had joined Jack in the stables, but they had still come to his mother's planned entertainments—until now.

"It really is the finest thing on four wheels I've ever seen," agreed Blair warmly. "And as fast as the wind, he assured us all."

He glanced sideways at his cousin. "So you're a member of his band of refugees?"

"I was merely investigating where all the port seemed to have disappeared to," replied Blair with a perfectly straight face.

"He took the best spirits, didn't he?" That explained things a bit more.

Blair just grinned again.

Gareth shook his head. "God help the woman Jack marries. She had better be made of stern stuff."

His cousin coughed. "We cannot all be as fortunate as you, Wessex, to marry a lady as agreeable as Miss Grey."

Gareth had nothing to say to that. Helen Grey *was* agreeable—perfectly, completely, alarmingly agreeable. Whatever he said to her, she agreed with. Whatever he suggested, she did. He was developing the oddest feeling that she was afraid of him. Even Withers opposed him from time to time, and Withers was his employee. He reminded himself to pay attention to her today—and then felt guilty that he was in any danger of overlooking her.

Perhaps if he had no interest in any of the women, he wouldn't feel that way. Unfortunately, Cleo Barrows had come to the wedding, and he was not only uninterested in his actual bride, he was fascinated by her sister. It was wrong. It was almost immoral. He wanted it to stop and yet felt helpless to do so when his eyes seemed to follow her of their own volition and his ears seemed more attuned to the sound of her voice than to any other's.

They reached the largest of the awnings, set on a gentle rise overlooking the bowling green. His mother came to meet them. "What a lovely surprise!"

"Isn't it my duty as a host?" Gareth kissed her cheek even as he covertly scanned the tent. He saw Cleo Barrows first, sending his heart leaping. She was speaking to another lady . . . whom he recognized a moment later as his betrothed bride. Not a promising beginning.

"I merely remembered that you told me you would be busy until the ball," his mother murmured, linking her arm through his. "I'm very pleased to see you were drawn out earlier." They strolled among the guests, pausing now and then to speak to someone. If Jack had assembled a gentlemen's retreat in the stables, it seemed his mother had created one under the awnings for the ladies. Round tables held pitchers of lemonade, plates of cakes and biscuits, and pots of tea, constantly refreshed by servants. The seating included small settees and benches, although Sophronia was sitting in a large upholstered chair, like a monarch on a throne, slicing a cheese with her sharp little knife.

"Finally come to see the girl, Wessex?" The old lady fixed her gleaming gaze upon him. "You've hardly spoken to your bride."

"Sophronia," said the duchess. "Really!"

"I came to see you," Gareth said before his mother could go on. He leaned down to kiss her cheek, which she presented with the regal detachment of a queen. "How are you, old dear?"

"Bored," Sophronia replied. "Everyone here is too polite. There's no trouble. No scandal."

"Do we really want that?" he asked mildly. It only encouraged Sophronia when people gasped and swooned at her outbursts.

"It's dull," announced the old lady, pointing her dirk at him. "What good is a house party if everyone's going to behave? I got my hopes raised when you invited that scamp, Jack Willoughby, but he's barely shown his face around here! And even worse, he's been a horrible distraction to Henrietta, and I have to let some parlor maid help me. I'm astonished to see her here today." She glanced over at Henrietta, who was holding a plate of cakes and listening with obviously strained patience to a very earnest-looking young woman. "She still hasn't brought my cake, though. I wager she'd bring it quickly enough if Willoughby wandered in."

"I will speak to Henrietta," began the duchess quickly, but Sophronia waved her off.

"Oh, let her have some fun. I'm sure they're up to something scandalous. I'd pay a shilling to watch them torment each other, but they keep disappearing and Henrietta refuses to tell me what they get up to, the vexing creature," she finished sourly, as if Jack and Henrietta had purposely schemed to deprive her of entertainment. "If she's going to desert me, she might as well tell me how naughty he can be."

"I'm not certain I can help," Gareth said. He doubted Jack would be flushed out of the stables by anything less than a duel.

"I daresay you can't," she grumbled. "Too upstanding by half. And your bride—Miss Grey! I never met such a polite, proper girl in my life. At least the party includes a few interesting people. Have you met Angela?"

Gareth glanced at his mother, who looked nonplussed. "I don't recall anyone by that name," she murmured.

"Oh! I invited her. The daughter of a very distant relation —not your side of the family, Alice. Very intriguing girl. She must have slipped off somewhere, but you'll meet her eventually." There was a hint of relish in the old lady's voice that made Gareth wonder what trouble this distant relation Angela might unleash.

"But Sophronia," said the duchess delicately. "The house is very full. I'm afraid we haven't any rooms to spare. If you had informed me earlier you wished to invite someone—"

"Don't worry about that," interrupted Sophronia. "Angela is staying with me. I need someone to talk to, now that Henrietta's set her cap for Willoughby." She scowled. "And if he doesn't recognize her for the prize she is, I shall take my dirk to him. He won't make a fool of my companion, no matter how charming his smile!" She stabbed her knife into the cheese for emphasis.

Gareth bit his cheek to keep from roaring with laughter at the image of Sophronia pursuing Jack with her dagger drawn. It was almost as entertaining as the thought of Jack falling for Henrietta, who was everything Jack was not: organized, responsible, and punctual.

He excused himself and made his way toward Helen, determinedly keeping his gaze fixed on her. She looked far livelier today, laughing and talking with obvious pleasure. She was truly lovely; her eyes glowed and there was a very handsome blush on her cheeks. She fluttered her hands about, as though portraying birds, and Gareth made the mistake of letting his eyes follow one graceful hand as she fluttered it over to rest on her sister's arm. Her sister, sitting very close to James Blair on the bench.

He almost missed his footing at the expression on Cleo Barrows's face. Her face was scrunched up with laughter— she had even wrinkled her nose—as she shook her head at whatever her sister said. Her curls bounced and threatened to topple down her back; one had already come loose and brushed the nape of her neck. Her sister was beautiful, but Cleo . . . she was captivating.

He had the growing feeling that he was doomed. The harder he tried to find a reason why she was undesirable in any way, the less success he had. He wanted to wind that loose curl around his fingers. He wanted to press his lips to the back of her neck, and the base of her throat. He wanted to talk to her, to have those sparkling brown eyes fixed on him, to see that impish grin directed his way. Instead he watched Blair receive all that and more when she turned to his cousin, put her hand on his arm, and leaned close to whisper something that made Blair throw back his head and shout with laughter.

"I'm delighted to see Miss Grey looking well again," said his mother. "I do believe Mrs. Barrows could make anyone smile, though."

He watched the way she tipped her head to one side, and for a single heartbeat their gazes met. "Indeed."

"James seems quite taken with her," his mother went on. "I understand she's a widow with a pretty income. He could certainly do worse, if he's thinking of marrying."

This time there was no mistaking the feeling oozing through his veins. It was jealousy, raw and bitter. It was utterly irrational and yet undeniable. He forced it down. "I suppose," he replied, in what he hoped was an offhand voice. "Has he said anything to you about her?"

"Of course not. Do you think I should encourage him?"

He gritted his teeth. "I think he's a grown man capable of deciding such a thing himself." Without waiting for her reply, he went down to join the boys still arguing over bowls. The only other male about seemed to be Blair, and Gareth found he had no patience to watch his cousin flirt with Cleo.

And he didn't swerve from his course when he saw the lady in question stroll down to the green ahead of him.

To Cleo's immense relief, Helen seemed like herself again when they walked down to the awnings the morning of the bowling party. Anyone's nerves would have been strained by their mother's incessant chattering about how grand and elegant everything—and everyone—was at the party. Cleo had long since grown content with what she could afford, but Helen had never been allowed to do the same. Sir William refused to acknowledge his straitened circumstances, and Millicent was incapable of economy; they had relied on Helen making a marvelous marriage to restore their fortunes. Cleo was fairly certain that burden had put the faint lines around her sister's mouth and brought a shadow to her eyes.

But the bowling party had revived her. Perhaps it was the weather, which had been nothing short of perfect. A group of young ladies, including the duke's sisters, had amused them for some time before Lady Sophronia came to grace them with her presence. Helen obviously found the old lady somewhat intimidating, but Cleo thought she was splendid. Sophronia spoke her mind and did as she pleased. When she'd had enough conversation, she simply announced that she was leaving.

"I see a fine cheese over there and want to secure it before someone else makes off with it," she confided. "The guests at these parties are like wolves, eating up every crumb in sight."

"Oh! May I fetch it for you?" Cleo offered, privately entertained by the description of the aristocratic guests as hungry scavengers.

"No, no. I can take care of myself." Lady Sophronia drew —of all things—a small pointed dagger from her pocket. "A memento of my third fiancé, Malcolm MacBride," she said fondly, showing them the knife. "I was very sad when the consumption took him. Still, it's a very useful dirk—that's what the Scots call it. I recommend you get one. No one interferes with a lady who is armed."

"No, I imagine not." Cleo's voice shook as the old lady nodded to them and hobbled after her cheese. She glanced at her sister and saw Helen's eyes tearing up. "Shall I give you a knife as a wedding gift, Helen?" she asked mischievously. "I don't want you to lose out on any fine cheese . . ."

Helen covered her face. "Oh, my," she gasped, fighting back giggles. "I can only imagine what Mama would say!" They were still shaking with suppressed laughter when Mr. Blair joined them. He immediately inquired what had made them laugh so hard, and Helen told him with animation and spirit, laughing anew at Sophronia's concern for her cheese. It made Cleo's heart lift to see her sister happy again. The only thing that might have pleased her more was if Wessex himself had joined them. He had arrived at the party with Mr. Blair, but was intercepted by the duchess. Cleo kept stealing glances at him, willing him to come over to them. He was looking fondly at Sophronia, and it was hard not to notice how attractive it made him. She wondered if he knew about Sophronia's dirk.

Then, by chance, their eyes met. It was just a passing glance, no more than a moment, but it sent a little shock through her. He was smiling, his dark eyes bright with mirth, and it transformed his face from handsome to mesmerizing. Cleo turned instantly back to Mr. Blair, but she could feel the duke's gaze upon her. It made her heart beat a little faster even as it reminded her of her vow to be quiet and discreet around His Grace. Helen had been right about one thing the other day: Cleo was more ebullient than her sister. She tended to attract people's attention. Therefore, she must absent herself when the duke and Helen met, so there could be nothing to distract Wessex from falling in love with Helen.

If it also kept Cleo from becoming more attracted to him, she would be immensely relieved.

When she caught the duke and his mother watching their little group, she murmured an excuse and slipped away. Mr. Blair was charming and had already brought a wide smile to Helen's face with an amusing story about Lady Sophronia; apparently, the dirk was not her only memento of a former suitor. Cleo knew her sister looked her best today, and if she left, the duke would be able to sit next to Helen and notice how enchanting she was.

Cleo walked down the gentle slope toward the bowling green, where two boys had been arguing for some time. "It seems you're in need of an umpire," she said as she reached them. "May I serve?"

"He put his foot in front of my bowl," said the younger boy at once. He was sturdy and blond, with the look of a boy who spent hours outdoors. "His bowl is dead and I ought to be allowed to replay mine."

"I did not!" Henry Ascot's eyes glittered with tears. "I never touched your bowl! It stopped on its own!"

"You did," accused the other. "And now you're trying to cheat!"

"I am not a cheat." His voice quivered, and Cleo could see how desperately he was trying to contain himself.

"'Cheat' is a dangerous word," she admonished them both. "One should never cast it about without proof. Do you have proof that he impeded your bowl? I presume you've measured every cast so far."

The first boy clamped his mouth shut and dropped the bowl in his hand. "Beg pardon, ma'am. I guess we ought not to play anymore." He ducked his head and walked away.

Cleo stooped to pick up the discarded bowl, giving Henry a moment to collect himself. He was tall and a bit gangly, with an uncompromisingly square brow and dark hair. Lady Bridget had called him a horrid pest, but he didn't look very dreadful now. "I hope there wasn't a wager riding on the match," she said.

He sniffed. "No. Not one I could win, at any rate." She glanced at him through her eyelashes. The poor boy looked thoroughly dejected. "I never win at bowls," he added softly.

"There's more to life than bowls."

"I know. There's boxing and racing and quoits and all manner of sport where I can be a disappointment to my father."

Cleo bit her lip. She knew more than a little about that herself. Before she could reply, though, someone else did.

"Every man has his talents, Henry. I daresay yours will turn out to be of far greater import than bowls."

Henry looked warily at the Duke of Wessex, who had walked up behind Cleo. "Do you really think so, sir?"

"I wouldn't say so otherwise."

"Of course not." The boy blushed. He shifted his weight, then awkwardly offered Cleo the bowl in his hand. "Thank you, ma'am, for settling things. I think I'd rather take a walk. Do—do you happen to know where my sister Charlotte's gone?"

"I'm sorry, no," said Cleo. Charlotte had disappeared with the rest of the young ladies some time ago, very soon after Henry and the other boy had reached the green.

"Toward the lake," said the duke. "I believe she was with my sisters."

Henry's dark eyes lit up, and Cleo got the idea he'd be quite a handsome fellow in a few years. "Thank you, sir!" He hurried off with a spring in his step.

"What a devoted brother, wanting to see his sister," she said lightly.

"Perhaps," replied the duke with a wry look. "I suspect it's more of an urge to torment. After I sent them back to the house the other day, Bridget came to me to lodge an indignant complaint that he had got mud on them."

"The things a man will do for love." Cleo heaved a dramatic sigh. "I'll wager a shilling he has a bad case of calf love for one of them."

"It had better not be Bridget." Wessex shuddered. "I had to order her not to put treacle in his bed. She didn't take it well when he ruined her favorite dress."

Cleo laughed. She started down the green to collect the abandoned bowls. "Have they really gone toward the lake?"

"I did see a group of young ladies in the general vicinity of the lake today," he confirmed, walking beside her. "It might have been some time ago . . ." Cleo laughed again. "But a long walk will do him good. He ought to clear his mind before he finds them. I've rarely seen one girl this week without three or four others nearby; the poor lad will be severely outnumbered."

"It builds character," she said.

"He'll need it if he fancies Bridget. I daresay she'll make Sophronia look demure and quiet."

"Yes. Lady Sophronia showed me her dirk." Cleo grinned at the way he cast his eyes upward and sighed. "A rather unusual remembrance of an old love."

"There are many unusual things about Sophronia."

"She is your great-aunt, I understand?"

The duke paused. "Great-great-aunt. Perhaps. I'm not entirely certain. I think I inherited her along with the house."

Cleo snorted with laughter, and this time he laughed, too. Something seemed to melt inside her at the sound. His laugh was a rough rumble, as if he didn't use it often. She stooped to retrieve a pair of bowls, holding them to her chest. When she rose, Wessex was holding the jack. He gave it a little toss, catching it easily in one hand. "Would you fancy a match, Mrs. Barrows?"

Cleo watched his fingers curve around the bowl. Good heavens, he had fine hands. "I haven't played bowls in a very long time."

"Neither have I," he said. "But it's a fine day out, and the greens are marked."

She glanced at the awning on the hill above as they walked to the head of the green. Helen was still in conversation with Mr. Blair, but she raised her hand and gave a cheery wave. Cleo was torn. It was a fine day, and she wouldn't mind a lighthearted game in the sun. Since the duke had invited her, surely not even her father would find it objectionable. She could suggest inviting Helen and Mr. Blair to join them, except that she knew her sister hated bowls. And perhaps this was her chance to determine the duke's feelings for Helen.

"Very well. But we must have stakes." She grinned at his raised brow. "Not money! After each cast, the winner must share something of himself or herself. After all, we shall be family within the week, and we ought to become acquainted, don't you think?"

He looked at her for a long moment. In the sunlight, his hair seemed to have a hint of auburn; the breeze had ruffled it until he looked quite tousled. And his eyes were so dark, unfathomably deep as he regarded her. Cleo heard the echo of her own words—*we shall be family*—and felt her heart sink a little. Oh, why had he followed her, thwarting her intent to avoid him? He ought to be sitting beside Helen right now, gazing at Helen, making Helen yearn to smooth his wild mane and imagine his large hands on her skin.

"Of course." Wessex bowed his head. "Will you set the jack?"

Unnerved, she turned toward the green and pitched the jack. It didn't roll far enough, and she clenched her hands as he strode out to get it. She had to wrench her gaze away as he bent over to pick it up; good heavens, he was a finely made man, from all angles. And he would be her brother. Sisters did not look on their brothers so admiringly.

The second time she managed to set the mark appropriately, and the duke stepped to the footer to cast his first bowl. "Were you a good bowls player, when you last played?"

Cleo laughed. "Oh, my. I certainly thought so, but I was a girl then." She delivered her first bowl, pleased to see it roll to within a respectable distance of the jack. Nearer than his, in fact. "I suppose you're far more accomplished, given that you have a bowling green within sight of your house."

He made his next shot. "Merely having a green doesn't make one skilled." His bowl wobbled off the green into the ditch.

"It takes a while to learn the bias of the bowls," she said diplomatically, hefting her own. It was smooth and dark, shaped more like a fat egg than a round ball. This time she misjudged, and the bowl came to rest at the edge of the green.

They played the rest of the end and then walked down

together to score it. "One point to you," said Wessex, collecting the bowls. "What secret do you want to tell me?"

"Se-Secret?" she stammered, laughing nervously. "Oh, no, I didn't mean a secret—"

"But we've only just met," he said, watching her in that too-intent way he had. "Everything about you is a mystery."

"Helen and I had a game, as children," she said after a moment. "We would choose a play—one of the great works of antiquity, most often—and act out every part. It nearly killed my father when we performed *Lysistrata*, even though Helen and I had very little idea what it was about."

"How old were you?" he asked, looking a little incredulous.

"About twelve," she said airily. "And Helen only eight."

Wessex coughed, then he laughed. "I would pay a fortune to have seen your father's face. He doesn't seem the type to take it well."

Her father didn't take most things she did well. Cleo's smile faded. "I was a bad influence even then," she murmured before she could stop herself. The duke gave her a keen glance but said nothing.

They bowled another end, and this time Wessex won a point. Cleo shook her head as she retrieved two of her bowls from the ditch but was glad that it was his turn to reveal something. "I inherited my title when I was sixteen," he said. "Barely older than young Henry." Her eyes rounded in shock. "My sisters were infants, my mother was heartbroken, and I was responsible for everything." He turned to face the house, squinting against the sun. "I was deathly afraid of letting my father down by making a hash of it."

"I'm sure he would be very proud!" Impulsively she laid her hand on his arm. "Kingstag is beautifully maintained. Your sisters are lovely young ladies, and it's clear to all that they adore you. No man can be a failure if his family loves him."

His arm flexed under her fingers. "Thank you," he said quietly. "My sisters' happiness is very important to me." He paused. "As is, I think, your sister's to you."

Cleo snatched her hand away. "Yes, very important." She went back to the mat, trying to ignore the faint question in his voice at the end. Helen's happiness *was* very important to her, and yet here she was, almost flirting with her sister's fiancé. She turned toward the awning again, both relieved and disconcerted to see Helen still absorbed in conversation with Mr. Blair. It should be Wessex sitting there with his head next to Helen's, bringing that glowing smile to her face. He should want to be there, instead of here in the sun with Cleo. But when the duke joined her, bowls in hand, she didn't say anything. She put her foot on the mat and bowled.

Wessex won another point. They walked to retrieve the bowls and she was glad again she didn't have to say anything. "What can I tell you?" he murmured, facing her thoughtfully. "Hmm."

"Something from when you were young," she suggested, thinking it would be safer. "A fond memory."

"Ah." He grinned. The wind lifted his hair from his forehead, and he looked boyish for a moment. "Blair came to Kingstag when he was about ten. His family fell on hard times and my mother invited him; his mother is her cousin. As you might imagine, we had a grand time, two boys with all this to explore." He swept one hand in a wide arc to encompass all of Kingstag. "One day I conceived a plan to go boating on the lake. Blair wasn't as eager but he went along with it, and we soon were in the middle of the lake, two sporting gentlemen at leisure." He shook his head. "Imagine my shock when I looked down to see an inch of water in the bottom of the boat. We neither of us wanted to swim—my mother would have punished us for spoiling our clothes and boots, to say nothing of taking out an old, leaky boat—so Blair bailed water with his hands while I rowed ferociously.

We managed to come within a few feet of the shore before it sank entirely. Both of us had the most incredible blisters."

"That's your fond memory?" Cleo smiled. "Blisters!"

"No, it was the thrill of saving ourselves from disaster."

"That I can understand, particularly if you didn't get caught."

"We didn't," he assured her, his eyes twinkling. "Blair and I have always backed each other up."

She laughed. "All the sweeter!"

"Indeed. It was one of the few times I truly escaped responsibility." He met her gaze. "Today seems like another. I can't say when I've enjoyed myself so much."

Cleo's heart felt warm and light even as she tried to tell herself he was just being polite. "Nor I, Your Grace."

"Wessex," he said. "Please."

Now her face felt warm. "Very well. But you must call me Cleo. After all, we shall be family." Perhaps if she reminded herself of that, forcefully and frequently, it would blunt the attraction she felt.

The expression on his face certainly didn't. If anything, it made things worse. Wessex had a way of looking at her that made the breath almost stop in her chest. "Very well, if you wish," he said after a moment. "Cleo."

She shouldn't have. She'd made a mistake. It sounded too familiar, too tender when he said it. Cleo glanced back at her sister in despair. Helen hadn't looked at Wessex any more than Wessex had looked at Helen. Not only had Cleo failed to discover the duke's feelings for her sister, she had only succeeded in making her own feelings worse.

If she didn't catch herself soon, she would find herself utterly in love with him.

As soon as possible, Gareth excused himself and went in search of oblivion. He found it in the stables. His cousin had the right idea, avoiding all the females. Some of the men looked a trifle guilty—Lord Warnford hastily hid a pair of dice behind his back—but Gareth just raised his hand in greeting and retired to a corner to contemplate the trouble he was in, a bottle in hand.

He brooded over his brandy while a tedious conversation about a horse race occupied the other men. The only person who appeared less interested in the race was the Earl of Bruton, who arrived shortly after he did and looked as grim as Gareth felt. He caught his old friend's eye and invited him to have a drink, not surprised to see Bruton here. With that slashing scar down his face, the earl had long avoided the ladies.

"Thank God for Willoughby," cried one decidedly drunk fellow all of a sudden. "He's saved us all with this refuge from the ladies."

"Hear, hear!" cheered the rest of the company.

"No offense intended, Wessex," added the man, still swinging his tankard of ale in one hand. "Felicitations on your marriage."

God help him; even drinking in the stables couldn't save him from that topic. He nodded in acknowledgement and poured another gulp of brandy down his throat, wondering if he could drink enough to purge the sound of Cleopatra Barrows's laughter from his mind. He could still feel the touch of her hand on his arm.

He left the stables, handing his bottle to Lord Everett as he went. If they raised a toast to his bride, he might be ill. There was one inescapable thought circling his brain, and he didn't know how to address it.

He was marrying the wrong woman.

❧ 8 ❧

C leo went downstairs early two mornings before the wedding, which was finally almost at hand. After their match of bowls, she had taken care only to cross the Duke of Wessex's path in company. Even at the ball last night, she had determinedly kept her distance. It hadn't kept her from noticing how very attractive he was, or how kind and good-humored he was with his sisters, or even how gallant he was to Sophronia. How could one dislike a man who was so wonderful? Cleo had clung to her sister's side and tried to interest herself in the wedding plans, but that had difficulties of its own. She thought she might scream if she didn't escape her mother's hawk-like watch for a few hours. As the wedding drew nearer, so apparently did her fear that Cleo would say or do something unacceptable.

Since Cleo knew very well that she was doing something unpardonable, it was hard to argue with her mother. She had diligently avoided talking about her shop except when directly asked, but her real sin was far worse, even though her mother could have no idea. She had tried everything to keep her wicked thoughts in check, to no avail, and now she had only one option left: avoidance. If she spent her time wandering alone over the estate and secluded herself in her room the rest of the time, she could endure until the wedding was over. Then it would be perfectly acceptable to make her excuses and return home to her little shop, where she couldn't ruin anyone's life but her own.

She paused before a mirror in the hall to tie her bonnet ribbons. The castle was still almost silent, populated only by the servants moving quietly about. Everyone would probably sleep late after the ball the previous night. In spite of everything, she would be sorry to leave Kingstag. It really was a wonderful place.

"Good morning," said a voice behind her.

Cleo jumped. The one voice she'd been trying to avoid but somehow still longed to hear. "Good morning, Your Grace," she managed to say, knotting her ribbons before facing him. "I was just setting out to indulge myself with a long walk."

"As was I." He wore a long coat and carried a rather battered hat. Cleo's pulse leaped as he pushed one bare hand through his thick dark hair. "I rarely have the time to step out later in the day."

"Oh! Please don't let me disturb you," she began, but he raised one hand.

"On the contrary. I didn't expect to meet anyone this morning, but it would be a pleasure to have company."

She should say no. She drew an unsteady breath. "I hate to disoblige you . . ."

"Please," he said, and Cleo closed her mouth. Without another word she put her hand on the arm he offered, and together they walked out the door.

A blanket of mist covered the ground, lending an unearthly air to the scene. Cleo drew in a delighted breath, loving the cool, earthy scent of the country. They strolled along the gravel, heading toward the lake, which lay still and quiet beyond the fog. "How beautiful," she sighed. "I rarely see such a sight in town."

"Are you always an early riser?"

She blushed. She had to be awake early to open the shop. "Yes. I love the morning light."

"My sisters and mother prefer not to rise until the sun is high in the sky."

"I'm sure they have good reason, particularly today," she said lightly. "It would be very hard to rise early when there are guests and entertainments every evening."

He smiled. "They are creatures of candlelight, even when there are no guests."

"As long as they are all the same, I see no cause for worry. If Bridget were to favor the morning while the others did not . . ." She shook her head and sighed as the duke chuckled. "It's lovely to see sisters so close."

"Barely three years separate them. My father was away for much of my childhood as a diplomat." Wessex slanted her a look. "My mother was quite joyous at his return."

Cleo sighed, but with a smile. "How lovely to find a married couple in love."

"And how sad when they are parted too soon," he murmured.

She said nothing. It was true. The last time she had walked arm-in-arm with a man had been two years ago, before Matthew was cut down by an inflammation in his lungs. Not since then had she ever once felt the same easy companionship she seemed to have fallen into overnight with the Duke of Wessex. He was nothing like Matthew and yet . . . in some ways he reminded her of her husband. He had a wry way of putting things. He was even-tempered with everyone, from his ebullient sister Bridget to Cleo's own flighty mother; even querulous Lady Sophronia never ruffled him. And he had a way of looking at her that made her feel every lonely minute of her widowhood.

"I understand you know too well how sad that is," he said quietly. "Forgive me for mentioning—"

"No!" She squeezed his arm lightly. "I have nothing but happy memories of my husband."

"Does that make it better or worse?" He cleared his throat. "To have loved and lost, I mean. My mother was destroyed when my father died. I was only a boy, but I became utterly convinced she would have been far happier if she hadn't loved him."

"I suspect she would disagree," Cleo murmured. "Love is worth the risk."

"Yes," he said after a moment. "I am beginning to agree with that."

"I am as sure of that as I am sure the sun will rise in the east. I took a great risk and suffered a great loss, but I would do it all again. Real love is very much worth it."

"A great risk," he echoed, sounding pensive. "What do you mean?"

"I suppose there's no reason not to tell you," she said, keeping her gaze fixed on something in the distance. She was under orders not to tell him and yet the words spilled out. "Helen knows, after all, so you would be sure to hear of it eventually. I eloped when I was seventeen. My parents have never forgiven me."

He stopped, and she had to stop, too. Cleo realized how far she had to tilt her head back to meet his eyes. "As bad as that?"

The concern in his voice made her flush. He wasn't haughty and arrogant, looking down on her for keeping a shop—unlike her parents. The temptation was too much. "Oh, yes," she said with a rueful smile. "I'm only here on sufferance."

"Oh?" His voice was soft and warm, comforting and seductive.

"Yes," she barreled on. "He wasn't enormously wealthy, titled, or extremely famous; he was a merchant. And my parents have never recovered from the shame."

"I see." He leaned forward a little. "Why did you do it, then?"

She smiled wistfully. "Because I loved him. He made me laugh."

The duke seemed mesmerized for a moment. His face was so still and yet rapt.

Cleo supposed she had just displayed her common nature, impulsive and reckless, and gave a little shrug. "There is so much of life that must conform to duty or polite behavior, but I don't know how people endure it all if they aren't *happy*, or at least content. My parents were horrified that I would run off like a hoyden with no care for how it reflected on my family. I suppose they only wanted better for me, but I . . . I was happy. For that, I could endure any discomforts life brought."

"Yes," he said, as though very struck by her words. "How very wise you are."

"Oh! Not really." She blushed at the look he gave her, direct and probing. "Headstrong. Willful." Those had been two of the kinder words her father used.

"What is headstrong and willful in a woman is often called decisive and bold in a man." He took a deep breath. "I wish we had had this conversation several months ago. You have shown me a multitude of errors on my part."

They had passed the bowling green by now, the awnings still standing like lonely sentinels over the bare rinks. Cleo felt again the way her heart had turned over when Wessex grinned at her over the bowls, the breeze ruffling his hair. Why did it have to be her sister's fiancé who made her heart leap? "I'm sorry," she said softly. "That wasn't my desire."

"No!" He shook his head. "On the contrary. I've never shied away from my mistakes. I made a great many of them, inheriting a dukedom at so young an age. Humiliation is a powerful teacher. But I fear it also taught me some lessons too well, lessons I've only just realized were all wrong."

She fixed her gaze upon the ground, afraid of what he would say next and yet desperate to know. "How so?"

"My parents were devoted to each other. My father's death . . . it seemed to shatter my mother. To my horrified young eyes, all that love seemed to have turned into soul-rending anguish. I was sure I wanted no part of that in my own marriage, and I never met anyone who changed my mind—until you."

"Love in marriage is vital," she whispered. Her heart thudded dangerously.

"I am more and more persuaded of that." He stopped walking. "You must understand . . . I had the best of intentions when I courted your sister. I don't love her, but I fully expected to be an honorable, faithful husband to her—"

"Stop." Cleo put her hand over his mouth to stop him. Tears prickled in her eyes. "Don't say anything else. You can love her—you *will*. Helen is the most wonderful girl, it's impossible not to love her—"

Gently, tenderly, he covered her hand with his, moving her palm to his cheek. His eyes closed for a moment and he inhaled a long slow breath as he leaned into her touch. "But not in the right way." He opened his eyes and looked at her, his face stark with yearning.

Cleo wavered on her feet at the longing that stabbed through her. If he had been anyone else in the world, she would be in his arms right now. God help her, she still wanted to be. But Helen—Helen, her beloved sister—even if Helen didn't love him and he didn't love her, Cleo couldn't betray her sister that way.

"You have to try," she said, her voice trembling.

"I have." He sounded helpless.

She pulled away from him, recoiling a step even though he made no move to stop her. "Keep trying. You've not spent enough time with her—it's just a bit of madness—we've only just met—"

"I don't think a lifetime will be enough to change my feelings so dramatically."

"Nor mine." The words slipped out before she could stop them. She raised a trembling hand to her mouth as if to recall them, but it was too late; he had heard.

If Gareth hadn't understood his own feelings before then, there was no doubting them now. He had thought—suspected—that Cleo was as attracted as he was, but he hadn't known if she felt more. But as her words lingered in the air, confirming what he yearned for, it seemed as though the earth finally went still beneath his feet again. After days of being off balance, caught between disbelief and alarm that he was falling in love when it was almost too late, he found he finally knew what he wanted.

He had tried to love Helen, he really had. After the bowling match, he'd kept his distance from Cleo and paid more attention to his betrothed. It hadn't helped—if anything, it had only convinced him he'd made a terrible error. Helen was as lovely and sweet-tempered as he had originally thought, but she was also far quieter. She was reserved and polite with the guests, and more than once he saw her glance longingly out the window, as if she couldn't wait to escape the room. For the life of him he couldn't remember why he'd thought she would make a good duchess; of course one could learn it and grow into it, and his mother was ready and able to teach her, but he suspected it would take years for Helen to feel at ease as the Duchess of Wessex and mistress of Kingstag Castle.

But when he looked at Cleo, more and more he saw someone who would be a splendid duchess from the beginning. She knew all the guests within days. His mother remarked on her effortless conversation. His sisters, who had been so eager to meet Helen, had quickly switched their adoration to Cleo, with her bold and unusual clothes and friendly manner. Even Sophronia liked her, and Sophronia was the harshest critic Gareth had ever met. What's more, she was used to running a large business, overseeing more than a dozen men, and managing her own finances—much the same skills that would be required to run Kingstag. He doubted anything would daunt her, including him in his worst temper.

And then there was the way she made him feel. When she smiled at him, Gareth would swear he could still feel the electric tingle in the air, as if lightning had struck him anew. When she laughed, he wanted to kiss her. When she took his arm, he wanted to carry her off into the shrubbery. And when she put her fingers on his lips, he wanted to fall to his knees and make love to her on the spot.

But deciding what he wanted was only part of the difficulty. He knew what he would have to do, somehow. It would be unpleasant, no doubt, and he didn't quite know how to go about it, but this was a risk that was definitely worth the reward.

"Cleo." He took a step toward her. She turned her face away, biting her lip, but otherwise she didn't move. He took another step and reached for her hand. "Tell me what you want," he murmured.

"It doesn't matter what I want."

"It does to me." He edged a step closer. She smelled of roses, soft and beautiful. "I didn't believe in love, let alone love at first sight. I am torn in two, caught between what I want and what I've promised. Tell me what you want, darling, and I will move heaven and earth to do it."

"I want my sister to be happy."

"Only your sister?"

A shudder went through her. "No," she whispered despondently. "But how can this end well for everyone?"

His fingers tightened on hers. "I promise it will."

"How can you promise that?" She shook her head. She pulled her hand loose and finally turned to face him. There was no sparkle in her dark eyes now, no teasing curve to her lips. It was all he could do to keep from touching her. He wanted to hold her close and swear that everything would fall in place. Her unhappiness gutted him. "My parents—my sister—what will they think if you cry off? How could I cause such humiliation for my own wicked desires? Do you know what people will say about me, if you desert Helen for me? I can't, Your Grace."

"And what will your sister think of me if I marry her strictly out of duty?"

For a long moment she said nothing. "I hope you won't—I hope you'll be happy with her, and she with you. But I won't interfere in my sister's marriage." She turned and hurried away, her footsteps muffled in the fog.

Gareth watched until she disappeared around the trees before cursing under his breath. He had to think; he had to find a solution to please everyone. He had learned to be a duke at age sixteen, responsible for solving his problems and everyone else's. This was no different . . . merely his entire future happiness was at stake.

He was startled out of his thoughts by Blair, who came trudging across the lawn with a pistol case in hand. His cousin stopped short when he saw Gareth. "Wessex."

"Blair." Gareth stared at the case. "You look like a man on his way to a duel."

"The duel was at dawn." Blair looked troubled. "Bruton and Newnham."

"They're cousins," said Gareth in shock. "And the best of friends—or so I thought. What did they duel over?"

"Rosanne Lacy. Newnham was courting her, but judging from what I just witnessed, Bruton will be marrying her."

"What you just witnessed," he repeated.

"Miss Lacy flying across the field, barely dressed and sobbing as if her heart would break." Blair's face twisted. "She flung herself into Bruton's arms and I could see it in

Newnham's face. He loved her and yet knew he'd lost her. It takes a strong man to watch the woman you love marry another man."

He heard again Cleo's anguished voice, asking what her sister would think if he jilted Helen for her. Cleo loved him, but she couldn't betray her sister.

On the other hand, the notoriously aloof Earl of Bruton had somehow fallen in love with the girl his cousin was courting, and he'd found a way to marry her. Gareth ignored the matter of the duel and focused on the result, which was that Bruton was marrying the right woman for him.

Somehow Gareth had to do the same.

"I trust no one was hurt," he said. When Blair shook his head, Gareth added, "Excellent. Then it seems everything has worked out for the best."

His cousin jerked up his head and gave him a strange look. "You really think so?"

He nodded. "Absolutely. I must remember to wish Bruton happy. He certainly deserves it."

"I expect he and Miss Lacy will be very happy," said Blair slowly.

"Yes." Gareth grinned. "I expect so, too."

❦ 9 ❦

Cleo took the long way back to the house before shutting herself in her room for the rest of the day. The conversation with Wessex whirled round and round her brain until her head ached. Every accusation her father had hurled at her seemed to be proven: she *was* wicked and reckless and dangerous to her family. Not only had she fallen in love with her sister's fiancé, she had only by the very thinnest of threads held herself back from kissing him. She never should have walked out into the mist with him. She never should have bowled with him. She never should have come to Kingstag at all. She ate dinner in her room and sent for her trunk to begin packing, so she could leave as soon as the wedding was over.

She only ventured out of her room late at night, when the house was quiet at last. She couldn't sleep and thought a turn in the garden might soothe her spirits. It must be beautiful in the moonlight. But a muffled sound caught her ear as she passed her sister's room, and before she could reconsider, she tapped gently on the door. "Helen!" she whispered into the jamb. "Let me in!"

The door jerked open and Helen stared at her with wide,

wet eyes. She turned her face away, swiping her handkerchief over her face. "Cleo. You're still awake."

She felt a chill of guilt. The duke had hinted that he didn't want to go through with the wedding, and now Helen was crying. She stepped into the room and closed the door. "What's wrong?"

"Nothing!" Her sister folded the handkerchief into her pocket and went to sit on the sofa. She looked up, a wobbly smile on her face. "Nothing at all."

"I can see very well that something is wrong." She sat next to her sister. "Why are you crying?" A sudden fear gripped her. "His Grace didn't make you cry, did he?"

"I haven't seen him all day," said Helen, wringing her handkerchief and missing Cleo's breath of relief. "How could I, when Mama kept me in this room all day with the dressmaker fussing over my gown, and had Rivers put up my hair three different ways to see which was most flattering, and wouldn't even let me go down to dinner because she thought I looked pale? She told me I must keep up my strength because I'm to be mistress of a castle." Her face began to crumple.

"Oh my dear." Cleo bit her lip. "What brought all this on?"

Helen gripped her hands together in her lap. "The wedding, of course. She's determined that everything must be perfect, because otherwise His Grace will be disappointed or ashamed of me. I don't think I can be perfect anymore. I don't know if I can do . . . this." She waved one hand around the beautiful room, but obviously including everything about Kingstag.

In spite of herself, a poisonous weed of hope sprouted in Cleo's heart. "What do you mean, you don't know if you can do . . . this?" She waved one hand around as Helen had done.

Her sister sighed. "Being a duchess sounded so delightful: beautiful clothes and jewels, the highest society, never worrying about money or being received or given the cut direct. And it made Mama and Papa so happy—I cannot tell you how it eased their minds about everything when I accepted Wessex. I don't think I've ever seen them happier."

Cleo pressed her lips together. She was growing thoroughly tired of her parents' feelings. What sort of people grew happier at the cost of their children's joy? Because it was clear to see that Helen, whatever her original feelings about her marriage, was decidedly not happy now. And if Helen wasn't happy, perhaps she oughtn't to marry Wessex.

She couldn't bring herself to say such a thing, afraid of persuading her sister to do something she'd regret just because it suited Cleo's own wishes. But neither could she advise her sister to forge ahead regardless of her feelings. "But you are not happy."

Helen jumped up and paced away. "I know I should be. Most of the time, I've wanted to run into the woods and hide, even as everyone tells me how fortunate I am."

"Many brides have nerves," murmured Cleo.

Her sister nodded, nibbling her bottom lip. "Were you nervous, when you married? Are all brides?"

"All brides should be happy," said Cleo diplomatically. She hadn't been nervous, she'd been eager. Why, if she were in Helen's shoes, about to marry Wessex . . .

But she wasn't.

"Do you think I will be?"

She blinked at the question. "What?"

"Do you think I will be happy?" repeated her sister. "Married to the duke. Mama sees no other possibility—who could be unhappy, married to one of the richest dukes in England? —but you've always been honest with me. What do you think of him, Cleo?"

She sat like a woman turned to stone. How could she possibly answer that, after the traitorous longing that still stained her soul? Wessex was everything she thought a man ought to be, and more. He was the friend she longed for, the companion she had been without for so long, the lover she dreamt of at night. But he would never be hers. "He's very kind," she managed to say. "Handsome. Charming, in a wry sort of way. I think he'll be a good husband."

"But do you think I can be happy with him?" Helen seized her arm, her fingernails digging into Cleo's flesh. "Do you?"

Her heart broke at her sister's expression, anxious and yet hopeful. She swallowed hard. "It doesn't matter what I think," she said quietly. "Only you can know what your heart compels you to do. Your happiness is in your hands."

Helen's gaze bored into her. "Yes," she murmured. Her grip loosened on Cleo's arm as she turned away, her eyes growing distant. "Yes, it is. If I tell him—if I make him understand how I feel—he will have to listen. He did ask me to marry him, and a man doesn't do that lightly, does he? If I persuade him that all this is too much . . . Yes, I think he will understand. It's not too late, is it?"

"You mean . . . the wedding?" Cleo frowned a little. "Has it simply overwhelmed you?"

"Has it!" Helen gave a disbelieving laugh. "To no end! I have no idea who half these guests are, and if I have to listen much longer to Mama talk about how perfect Kingstag is and what an honor it is to be mistress of it, I may scream. You were so clever to elope, you know. You spared yourself immense aggravation." She stopped, looking startled, then flashed a cautious grin. "I shouldn't have said that, should I? Well, I think I'm done with doing what I ought to do."

"Oh," said Cleo, disconcerted. "Good."

Her sister laughed again. "It *is* good—or rather, it will be, thanks to you."

"I just want you to be happy," Cleo repeated. And she would do whatever it took, including going away and never visiting her sister and her too-tempting husband again.

Wessex was not hers to lose; he was Helen's. And Helen certainly wouldn't lose him to Cleo.

Helen smiled. Tears still glittered in the corners of her eyes, but they no longer ran down her cheeks. "You do, don't you? Oh, Cleo, I think I would have gone mad without you. Sometimes I feel as if you are the only one who truly understands me." She flung her arms around Cleo, and Cleo hugged her back, heartsick. If Helen really hadn't wanted to marry Wessex, there might have been a chance . . . But it was foolish to have let the thought cross her mind. Firmly she smothered it, renewing her silent vow to leave as soon as the wedding took place.

"There," she said, patting Helen's back. "Dry your eyes. You only have one more day before your wedding." The words were like a blow to her heart. "It's finally upon us," she said, her voice only breaking a little at the end.

Helen laughed, swiping at her eyes. "Yes. So it is—and I am ready for it at last," she said. Her doubts seemed to have been allayed, which meant they couldn't have been very serious doubts. Cleo told herself that was a good sign. "Thank you for coming. You've done me a world of good."

Helen mustn't know that her conscience was only just holding back the longing she felt. Helen didn't know her sister was thinking impure thoughts about her future husband. Cleo gave a shaky smile. "I'm delighted to be of help, any help I can be."

"Believe me," said Helen earnestly, "you've been more help than you know."

GARETH REALIZED TWO TRUTHS THAT DAY.

First, he couldn't marry Helen Grey. Not only did he not love her—and suspect she did not love him—but the mere mention of Cleo made him forget the very existence of his betrothed bride. Just a glimpse of her snared his attention, and the very sound of her voice made him deaf to anything and anyone else around him. Everything she did persuaded him she would be perfect as his duchess—not a biddable ornament but a true partner. Gareth had little choice but to admit he was utterly lost.

But second, Cleo would never do anything to hurt her sister, even if she did want him as badly as he wanted her. What could he say to that? Gareth had sisters, too. He would never want to hurt them. Still, it would hurt Helen far worse to end up married to the wrong man, and he knew he must speak to her. Somehow—without mentioning Cleo—he would persuade her to break it off. It would be a great surprise to all the guests, but he was sure his family would support him, particularly when he revealed his true affection to them.

But there his plans were thwarted. For the rest of that day, Helen seemed to have gone into hiding. He finally located Sir William and inquired, only to be told Helen was busy with her mother, having her dress fitted. Mention of the wedding gown only made Gareth more anxious to see her, but she wasn't at dinner. Neither was Cleo. He went to bed determined to see both of them the next day.

He hadn't counted on his own mother and sisters, who surprised him with a private family breakfast the next morning in the duchess's sitting room. "After today you will belong with your wife," his mother told him with a smile as they lingered over coffee, "but we wanted you to ourselves one last time."

"I refuse to give you all up," he replied. "Surely you're not planning to leave after tomorrow?"

Serena laughed. "Of course not! But you won't want us about anymore, when you have Miss Grey."

Gareth had to bite his tongue to keep from correcting her. "I shall always want you about. Who else will protect me from Sophronia? She was threatening Jack with her dirk the other day."

Bridget hooted. "Perhaps Mrs. Barrows will! She's not frightened of Sophronia."

An excellent idea, thought Gareth, sipping his coffee to hide his reaction to her name. He quite liked the idea of Cleo defending him.

"Come, girls." The duchess rose from her chair. "Your brother has a great deal to do before the wedding tomorrow. We must leave him in peace." They protested a little, but bade him farewell with much laughing and teasing.

He turned to his mother as the girls trooped out. "May I ask a question, Mother?"

"Of course," she said in surprise.

Gareth took a deep breath. "Would you have married Father if you had known how little time you would have together?"

Her lips parted. "Oh, my. Without a doubt. I loved him too much. A year with him made me happier than a lifetime with any other man could have done."

He nodded. "For years I thought otherwise, you know; that the pain of losing him was so great, you must have wished you had never loved him at all."

She put her hands on his arms and studied his face. "No. The love was greater than the pain." She hesitated. "I wish you every bit as much happiness, Gareth, and for many more years than I had."

"I thought you might say that." He kissed her cheek. "Thank you, Mother." He ought to have listened to her from the start, he realized, and set off to make her wish come true.

Unfortunately, his luck was no better this day than the last. By the time he found Helen and was able to manage a quiet word with her alone, everyone had gathered for dinner.

He drew her aside before they went into the dining room. "I must speak to you tonight."

She ducked her head. "Is it about tomorrow?"

"Er—yes."

Helen put her hand on his arm. Gareth remembered Cleo doing the same thing, although her touch had sent a shock of awareness through him, while Helen's only made him tense. "Your Grace, I want to speak to you as well. I think tomorrow will be difficult for us both, but you must know that I'm confident it will be for the best. I've been worried about the wedding, you see, but my sister helped me understand that it will lead to great happiness."

"Ah—yes. About that . . ."

"I want you to be happy," she said wistfully. "As much as I want my own happiness."

This was not going well. Gareth cleared his throat. "Will you meet me later tonight, then?"

She hesitated, and her mother swooped in. "Helen dearest! Oh, Your Grace!" She curtseyed, beaming from ear to ear. Gareth remembered the veiled hurt in Cleo's voice when she spoke of her parents and could barely bring himself to nod at Lady Grey. "What a lovely couple," she gushed. "I was just telling Lady Warnford how handsome you look together. I'm sure Sir William will hire a painter to capture your likenesses so we might always remember how perfect a pair you form!"

"There's no need to rush to do so. Mama, His Grace has just invited me to walk out after dinner. May I?"

Lady Grey gasped. "Indeed not! It's the night before the wedding! Not only is it bad luck, you need your rest, my dear! Please understand, Your Grace," she hastened to add. "You will have her every night after tonight!"

Gareth clenched his jaw as Helen demurely bowed her head. "Yes, Mama. I am sorry, Your Grace."

"Quite right," he said bitterly. How the bloody hell was he supposed to talk to her? He was the Duke of Wessex, damn it, and if he wanted to see his bride . . . in order to persuade her to jilt him . . . he ought to have the right to do so.

He barely paid attention at dinner, working out in his mind how best to present the problem. Cleo wasn't there again, for which he was grateful. There was still a stir over the engagement yesterday of Miss Rosanne Lacy to the Earl of Bruton, although no mention of the duel. Even Jack Willoughby's shocking announcement that he and Henrietta Black had agreed to marry only diverted Gareth for a moment. There were several rounds of toasts, and Sophronia declared that she'd suspected that match all along, but Gareth only saw the ring. After making a blushing Henrietta stand up with him, Jack had presented Gareth with the Cavendish heirloom ring that had been sent to London for cleaning and sizing. He was supposed to put that ring on Helen Grey's finger tomorrow morning. It sat on the table in front of him, taunting him through the port and the ribald conversation of the other gentlemen when the ladies had left. Every man here seemed pleased to be getting married except him.

By the time he extricated himself from the guests, Gareth was almost wild with impatience. He had to do this tonight. In the morning it would be too late; the bride would be dressing for a wedding he no longer wanted to happen. He finally decided to wait until the house was quiet and then go to her room. It was improper, but he didn't see any other way. He couldn't stand at the altar tomorrow beside Helen, all the while wishing it were Cleo standing beside him instead, Cleo with his ring on her finger, Cleo in his bed that night. Although if it were Cleo next to him, Gareth was quite certain she would be in his bed long before night. His mother could entertain the guests at the wedding breakfast, and he could entertain Cleo upstairs.

He retreated to his study and dropped into his chair with a sigh, letting his head fall back. He poured a generous glass of brandy and let his mind run wild with all sorts of schemes, in case he couldn't persuade Helen. He could pay Sir William to break the betrothal. At this point, any amount of money would be a small price to pay. He could invent some crisis in London he must attend to at once and literally flee the scene. He could shoot himself in some harmless place to buy time; a man with a bullet in his leg could hardly stand up in church. Gareth set down his empty glass with a thunk when he realized he was willing to cripple himself to avoid a wedding he had once sought. He glanced at the clock and cursed; he should wait another hour at least before seeking out Helen. He'd have no choice but to marry her if people saw him going into her bedchamber.

He lifted the glass, intending at least one more drink, and a letter came with it, stuck to the bottom. He pulled it off and started to toss it back on the desk when the direction caught his eye. It was to him, in Blair's hand. Gareth frowned. It hadn't been here earlier in the day. Blair hadn't said a word to him at dinner, or after. Gareth had bade him good-night barely an hour earlier. What would his cousin write that he couldn't say aloud? He broke the seal and unfolded the letter.

He read it three times before the meaning sank in. And then he began to smile. He read the letter again, just to reassure himself he understood it, then laughed out loud. What a prize Blair was! And what an idiot *he* was; if he hadn't been knocked senseless by Cleo's sly little smile, he surely would have noticed something earlier and deduced what had made Blair so quiet and bitter lately.

But how to proceed now? Gareth thought carefully for a moment, absently rotating the empty glass under his fingers. This would solve all his troubles, if handled properly, and not merely his own troubles. At last he got to his feet, folded the letter carefully into his pocket, and poured another drink, smaller this time. He raised the glass to the portrait of his father above the mantel. "To Cleopatra, your future daughter-in-law," he told the painting. "And to James Blair, the finest man I know."

❧ 10 ❧

The wedding day dawned cool and misty. Awake since before first light, Cleo lay staring at the ceiling until the maid brought warm water for her to wash. There would be dark circles under her eyes, but the last two days of solitary contemplation had been good for her, in a way. She had nothing to regret; she had lost nothing that had been hers. What she felt for Gareth . . . it was unnatural, besides being wrong. People couldn't fall in love so quickly, she told herself. It was not love; it was merely desire, or perhaps a hidden longing to be married again emerging with all the fuss over Helen's wedding. It would pass, she told herself, trying to believe it. Sooner or later. The important thing was that she hadn't acted on any of those mad, wicked impulses and betrayed her beloved sister.

She dressed slowly, carefully. Her mother had dictated her gown for the day, and Cleo had rolled her eyes behind her mother's back at the volume of lace and the bland shade of gray. It would have been entirely appropriate for elderly Lady Sophronia—or rather, for someone of Lady Sophronia's age, for Sophronia would probably have sliced the gray dress into pieces with her little Scottish dirk. Normally Cleo would feel the same way; Matthew had even made her swear not to wear mourning for him. He didn't want her to be old before her time, he had said. But this morning Cleo put on the gray dress without complaint. Today she felt old and mournful, and might as well look it.

She drank the tea the maid brought, then just sat by the window, staring blindly at the grounds. The carriages were to come at ten o'clock to carry them to the Kingstag chapel. It was only a little past eight, although if Cleo knew her mother, the carriages would be waiting at least half an hour. Millicent was incapable of being on time to anything.

A maid interrupted her morose thoughts. "Your pardon, ma'am, but your mother, Lady Grey, requests you come to her."

Cleo's eyebrows went up, but she went without question. No doubt she would provide an audience to her mother's raptures over Helen's gown and hair and shoes. With something as momentous as this, Millicent would need someone to boast to, and Cleo was the only person who would listen and not think her crass. She braced herself and tapped at Helen's door.

It opened and her mother seized her arm, whisking her inside before closing the door behind her. Cleo rubbed her arm, startled. "Why must you do that, Mama?"

"Shh!" Millicent pressed a handkerchief to her lips before her face crumpled. "Something awful has happened."

Her heart stopped. "What? Is Helen ill?"

"Helen," said her mother in tragic tones, "is not here."

"What do you mean? Of course she's here, somewhere at Kingstag." Cleo was astonished. "When did you discover she wasn't in her room? We must look for her—"

Millicent waved her handkerchief as if to dispel the words. "Don't say that! Would you have us run up and down the corridors calling her name? What would people think?"

"They'll notice if she doesn't come to her own wedding."

Cleo tried to tame her thoughts into order. "Chances are she woke early from nerves and went for a walk. Have you checked the garden?"

"Of course we did!" snapped her father, pacing in front of the fireplace. "What kind of fool do you think I am? I went there first thing."

"But she's not there—her bed hasn't been slept in—she never rang for her maid—she's gone and run off and we'll all be humiliated when His Grace discovers it!" Millicent burst into loud weeping. Cleo patted her mother's shoulder numbly, not knowing what to think. Where could Helen be? Had she truly run off?

Her heart took a mad leap at the thought; perhaps her sister didn't wish to marry Wessex after all. Perhaps there was a chance for Cleo to have him without hurting her sister and causing a scandal. She was a wicked woman for thinking it, but she did think it.

"We must tell His Grace," she began, only to be cut off by her father.

"We most certainly must not! What will he think?"

"He'll think Helen's not here," said Cleo, "which is true. Mama, we must tell him," she insisted as her mother shook her head and burst into tears again. "We cannot conceal her absence! He'll notice his bride is missing."

Millicent clutched at her arms. "You must find her," she begged. "Please look—you and she were always thick as thieves. We'll be a laughingstock if she jilts the Duke of Wessex at the altar!"

Cleo ignored that. She rather thought the duke wouldn't mind being jilted, but there might be another reason Helen had gone missing. "I'll go look for Helen, but I have to tell the duke. He has a right to know," she said, raising her voice as her mother began to moan softly. "Let me change my shoes and get a pelisse."

"Yes! Yes, you must go." Her mother retreated to the sofa. "Oh, where are my Smythson's Smelling Salts?"

Cleo went back to her own room and kicked off her gray satin slippers. Her sister might have gone for a walk and fallen; she could be lying hurt somewhere on the vast estate. Walking boots in hand, Cleo sat down at the dressing table, not bothering to ring for her maid to change her dress. Until she knew Helen was at least safe, there was no time to lose. She laced up one boot, combing her memory for any place Helen might have wandered. Where could she be?

The answer stared her in the face when she reached for the second boot.

Cleo seized the note tucked partly under a box of face powder. It was folded small and bore her initials in Helen's delicate writing. Unfolding it with shaking fingers, she read. Then she read again. She laughed a little madly, then stopped at once, glancing around the room in guilt. People would think she was mad, and Helen, too.

Oh, God. What a twist.

On shaking legs she went back to her mother's room. Her parents were where she had left them, alone, thank God. She closed the room door behind her, and cleared her throat.

"What is it?" barked her father.

"I've found a note," she said, "from Helen."

That roused even Millicent. "What does it say?" Sir William strode across the room to snatch the paper from Cleo's hand before she could read it. His eyes skimmed it, then his face blanched, and he thrust it back at her as if it burned him. "You!" he croaked. "You did this!"

"No!" she gasped. "No! I did nothing!"

"What?" cried Millicent, struggling off the sofa. "What has happened to poor Helen?"

"Poor Helen," spat Sir William, "has disgraced us all! Disgraced and ruined us! And you—" He shook his finger at Cleo. "You are responsible!"

"I most certainly am not!" Cleo's temper finally snapped at his unjust accusation. She had held her tongue about her shop and endured his suspicion without a word, but now she had had enough. "You are, Papa, if anyone is. You and Mama both."

He reared back. "How dare you!"

"Helen has been unhappy and anxious since we arrived, and neither of you paid any attention because you were so pleased she was marrying a duke. I knew she was unhappy, but she insisted it was just nerves—which you, Mama, made worse with your incessant talk of how glorious Kingstag is and what an honor it will be to preside over it."

"But it's a castle," protested her mother. "Helen needs to know—"

Cleo threw up one hand. "Helen needed to know her future husband cared for her. She needed to know she would be happy with him. It doesn't matter what sort of house he has if she's miserable!"

"This is the match of the season!" said her father furiously. "A brilliant marriage! You tempted your sister away from following her duty, prompting her into some hysterical fit. I knew it was a mistake to let you come."

She shook her head. "Why is it Helen's duty to replenish your fortune, Papa? Why wasn't it your duty to make economies or learn investments or do anything at all to support your family? Instead you've been content to live off your daughters, taking the money I earned in my hateful little shop and now selling Helen in marriage, regardless of her feelings in the matter."

Sir William's face was purple. "You are dead to me now."

Cleo just lifted one shoulder sadly. "I know. I've been dead to you for years. But now I think you shall be dead to me as well, if you cannot forgive Helen for what she's done. Being happy is more important than being a duchess." She turned to go.

"Cleo!" Her mother's anxious voice stopped her. "You—you will still try to find her, won't you? To make sure she's not hurt, and—" Millicent cast an anxious glance at her husband. Cleo's heart started to soften toward her mother. Perhaps one parent would be made to see reason; surely her mother still cared about more than Helen's status. "And perhaps," Millicent went on hesitantly, "perhaps she might reconsider . . ."

"Yes, Mama," she said, and left the room, closing the door on her parents. Her heart thudded, both with disbelief that she had finally been so blunt with them and with surprisingly little regret. She had borne it because she believed that, deep down, they loved her and Helen; she had told herself they were simply unable to conquer their disappointment in her marriage to Matthew. A shopkeeper was a distinct step down, and she had excused them that.

But finally she accepted that it was excessive pride, indifferent affection, and arrogance. They wanted their daughters to marry well so they might live more comfortably and trade on their daughters' connections. Her actions, like Helen's today, mattered to them only as a reflection on their own state.

And if Helen had finally taken charge of her own life and happiness, there was nothing at all to stop Cleo from doing the same. She didn't know where Wessex's rooms were, but she found the butler and told him she must speak to the duke urgently. He directed her to the study at the back of the house, overlooking the gardens.

At the door she took a deep breath and knocked. Just the sound of his muffled voice made her pulse jump. She let herself in, glancing quickly around to be certain there was no one else in the room.

He was alone, standing in front of the window with his hands clasped behind his back. Just the sight of him made her dizzy with yearning and hope. She unfolded Helen's note. "I have something to tell you, Your Grace. It is about my sister."

His attention was fixed on her. "Oh?"

"Yes." She checked that the door was securely closed. "My sister left me a note, which I only discovered a few minutes ago. May I share it with you?" He inclined his head, and she wet her lips, then read Helen's note. "*Dearest Cleo: By the time you read this, I shall be gone from Kingstag Castle. I am writing to you because you are the only one who will understand why: James and I are eloping. We hope to make Gretna Green by the end of the week.*"

Her voice faltered. She swallowed, and read on. "*I am very sorry to do such a thing to His Grace. He honored me greatly with his offer of marriage, and I did accept him honestly. But I feel it would be an even greater disservice to him if I were to go through with a marriage I no longer want, and could not be happy in, while I loved another man. Comfort him, Cleo, and tell him I am sorry. Your loving sister, Helen.*"

For a long moment there was silence. Cleo folded the note, unsure what to do next.

He crossed the room to her. "May I see it?" She gave it to him, trembling a little as his fingers brushed hers. Wessex unfolded the note and read it before letting it fall to the ground. "So I've been jilted."

"I believe you have been." Her heart beat so hard it hurt. He wasn't going to marry Helen, sang the wicked voice inside her head. Some remnant of duty obliged her to add, "My parents are distraught that Helen would do such a thing."

"Yes, I imagine they are," he murmured. "Are you?"

"Well—I wish my sister had confided in someone before disappearing in the night and giving us a great fright . . ."

"James Blair is the most capable man I know. If she's with him, she is perfectly well."

She just nodded, overwhelmed by the jumble of hope and uncertainty inside her. He was taking the news very calmly, but also without any show of the relief she felt that now he—like Cleo—was free to follow his heart. Perhaps his heart had reconsidered; perhaps he couldn't stomach the thought of anything to do with her family after Helen's action. She was a common merchant, after all, hardly a likely duchess. Perhaps she had been all wrong . . .

"And have you come to do as your sister asked?" He rested one hand against the door above her shoulder. "Have you come to console me, Cleo?"

The way he said her name was almost a caress. "If there is any way I can."

A smile bent his mouth as his eyes darkened. "I think I may require excessive consolation after this most distressing fortnight."

"And being jilted," she whispered.

His smile grew darker, more intimate. "My darling," he said, "being jilted has been the best part—thus far."

Cleo's knees went weak. She hadn't been wrong at all. She laid her hand on his chest. He was wonderfully big and warm beneath her palm, his heartbeat steady and strong. "Your heart doesn't seem broken."

He laid his hand over hers, pressing it against his silk waistcoat. "On the contrary—I think it has only just begun to beat with purpose, now that you are here."

She listed toward him. "Why is that?"

He smoothed a wisp of hair away from her temple, then curved his hand around her nape. "Because I can finally do this," he said, and kissed her.

She melted against him, opening her mouth and meeting his tongue with her own. She gripped his jacket, holding him to her, and then she forced the lapels wide, trying to peel it off him. With a harsh exclamation, he pulled his arms free of the jacket and let it fall to the floor behind him before gathering her close. She pressed against him, her cheek on his chest, listening to the rapid thump of his heart.

She could feel the warmth of his skin through his shirt-sleeves.

"Cleo," he murmured against her hair. "If there is any reason . . . any objection you have to me making love to you, tell me now."

"No," she gasped, catching his shoulders as his hands slid down around her bottom, lifting her up onto her toes, dragging her against his rigid arousal.

"No? I should stop?" He tugged her earlobe between his teeth.

Cleo whimpered. "Don't stop," she moaned. "Don't ever stop."

His hand slipped behind her back, pulling loose the tiny pearl buttons of her gown. The demure bodice slid down, and then he pulled it further down until her breasts were almost exposed. She shuddered at the cool air on her flesh, her head falling back against the door behind her. His hand cupped her breast, his mouth was hot on her neck. "Wessex," she gasped, dimly thinking they ought to find a more comfortable location.

"Gareth." He pulled at her bodice again, and there was a sound of cloth ripping. "My God, you're beautiful in every way." He lowered his head to her breast and Cleo abandoned all thought of moving. She plowed her fingers into his thick dark hair and gave herself up to the pleasure of his lips on her skin, his teeth scraping over her taut nipple, his tongue playing along the delicate flesh of her bosom.

He drew up the skirt of her gown, and she shifted her feet to allow him to press ever closer to her. He raised one eyebrow as his boot bumped against hers. Cleo blushed; in her hurry she'd run through the house wearing only one shoe. Gareth simply grinned as he fell to his knee, unlaced the boot, and tossed it aside, and then his hands were exploring the length of her legs. His fingers skimmed her silk stockings, plucked at her garters, and then roamed higher. She gasped aloud in pent-up desire when he finally touched the aching folds between her legs.

Even she, who had eloped at seventeen, had never been so careless of propriety and restraint. With inarticulate words and sighs she urged him on, clasping his head to her bosom as he stroked her and teased her. When her legs threatened to give out beneath her, she managed to tug at his hair. "Gareth," she gasped, her heart thundering and her breath ragged. "Gareth, please . . ."

He shuddered. "When you say my name that way . . ." He lurched to his feet, tearing at his trousers. "Put your arms around my neck," he commanded, his voice rough. Cleo obeyed, glad he put his own arm around her waist. She might have stumbled and fallen if he hadn't. "Now tell me . . ." He caught her knee and pulled, hooking it around his hip to hold her skirt out of the way. "Say you want me, Cleo . . . Please, darling . . ."

"I want you madly." She strained against him. "I want you now."

"Thank God." He cupped his hand around her bottom and held her as he fitted himself against her and pushed home. Cleo made a faint gasp of delight and surprise. It felt so good, so right, to have him inside her. She tightened her grip on his neck and pressed her forehead against his shoulder. Every nerve felt alive as he held her so easily, so securely, so intimately. He seemed as moved as she was. His chest heaved and his arms trembled. "At last," she thought he whispered, and then he began to move.

Whatever making love against a door might lack in finesse and comfort, Cleo thought she might prefer it to any other kind. She curled herself around Gareth, meeting each hard thrust with a little arch of her back. He held her easily, he knew right where to touch her, and when it all culminated in a fierce climax, she almost burst into tears. Gareth caught his breath and rested his forehead against hers as his hips jerked a few more times in his own release, and then he kissed her, leisurely and thoroughly.

And then there came a soft tap at the door. Cleo started in spite of the hazy contentment that enveloped her. She could feel the knock through the wood at her back, and the thought of what the person on the other side would think, if he knew what was just inches from him, made laughter bubble up in her throat. Lips pressed shut to hold it back, she looked up at Gareth, her eyes tearing.

He grinned lazily down at her. "Yes?" he called.

There was a pause, then the butler's voice came through the door, low and rushed, as if he were whispering through the crack of the doorjamb. "Your Grace, Mr. Blair wishes to see you at once."

The laughter stuck in her throat died. Cleo didn't move, her fingers clenching in the folds of Gareth's shirt. Mr. Blair had returned, which meant Helen must have as well.

Oh, Lord.

Gareth just kept smiling down at her. "Does he? Excellent. Where is he waiting?"

"In the stables, Your Grace. With Miss Grey."

"Ah. Tell them I shall be with them directly."

"Yes, sir." Cleo could hear his footsteps faintly, going down the hall. Gareth still wore the slight grin of a cat who knew where the cream was hidden, and she didn't know why. Part of her longed to run out to the stables and hug Helen close before shaking her and demanding an explanation, and part of her didn't want to face her sister for years. She had just made love to her sister's fiancé. Even though Helen hadn't wanted to marry him, she might still be shocked and horrified to hear how quickly he had turned to Cleo.

And now there wasn't much time for her to talk to Gareth before facing Helen. What did he want from her? Making love was one thing, but there were no promises between them.

Cleo wanted more. She didn't want to give him up to anyone, ever again.

She wet her lips. He was still inside her, his hand still curved around her hip. With a little wriggle, she unhooked her leg from around his, easing her weight back to the ground. With a soft sigh, he slid free of her, his hands steadying her waist as her knees wobbled. She smiled uneasily, smoothing down the skirts of her gown as Gareth repaired his own clothing. She wasn't sure she could stand under her own power. Even now, aftershocks of pleasure left her muscles lax.

"Cleo." His hand cupped her face, making her look at him. Gareth smiled. "You look so grim, darling. Was I that rough?"

Her mouth fell open. "No! You know you weren't. It was wonderful. But Gareth—" He cut her off with a long kiss, and when he lifted his head Cleo had forgotten what she'd been saying.

"All will be well," he said. "Trust me." She gazed up at him, afraid to ask. "You look as though a great problem troubles you," he added.

She was surprised into a weak laugh. "A great problem! This is a rather out-of-the-ordinary problem, I think . . ."

"Yes, I might have ruined this gown beyond repair." He gave it a frown. "Although it's not my favorite."

She blushed. "My mother chose it."

"No wonder," he muttered. "I won't apologize for ripping it, then." Still, he turned her around and fastened what buttons remained. "Will you come with me? I expect your sister will want to see you."

"What are you going to say to them?" she asked softly. His fingers moving so gently over her back had sapped her will to argue.

"I think your sister and my cousin explained themselves

very well in the notes they left. I can't think what they might have to add to that."

Cleo blinked and whirled around. "Your cousin left you a note as well?"

"He did."

"Then you knew before I told you that Helen had run off?"

"I did."

"You might have told me," she protested.

He grinned. "But I desperately wanted comforting, darling." He kissed her. "Let's go see what they have to tell us, shall we?"

G areth felt at great charity with the world as he and Cleo walked toward the stables. He held her hand in his; she had looked a bit self-conscious at first, but she made no effort to pull away. There was a beautiful flush on her cheeks, and her eyes sparkled as they had the morning she first arrived at Kingstag, when lightning had seemed to strike him in the head.

A servant lingering near the front gate ran forward to meet them and say that Mr. Blair was waiting in the rear tack room, where Jack Willoughby had established his gentlemen's refuge earlier. As they headed there, they passed Jack's shiny black phaeton, now covered with dust and being fussed over by a number of grooms. Cleo darted a curious look at him, but Gareth just shrugged. He had a feeling Hippolyta had helped the lovers in their escape and in their inexplicable return.

The instant they stepped through the door, Helen Grey jumped up from the bench. She was wearing traveling clothes, her hair swung in a braid down her back, and her eyes were haunted. On the bench behind her, James Blair sat with his hands on his knees, his head hanging as if exhausted.

Helen took a hesitant step forward, eyeing them almost fearfully.

Without a word, Cleo opened her arms, and Helen fell into them, breaking into ragged weeping. The sisters held each other close. Blair's expression twisted in anguish before he averted his face. Both were the picture of misery.

"I'm sorry," Helen sobbed. "I'm so sorry, Cleo. I didn't mean to cause trouble, but I was so unhappy and it seemed like the best idea . . ."

"Are you hurt?" Cleo pulled back to scrutinize her sister's face, red and puffy and tear-stained. "Are you well?"

She nodded. "I'm fine. We—James and I—we're both well. It's just—it's just—"

James Blair rose to his feet. "We both knew it to be wrong," he said, his voice hoarse. "Wessex—Mrs. Barrows—I cannot apologize enough for what we've put you through. It was entirely my doing. I convinced Miss Grey—"

"No! I convinced him!" Helen grasped her sister's hands. "It was my idea, all mine! I couldn't go through with it. Cleo, you told me my happiness was in my hands and you were right, you truly were. I found James yesterday and forced him to take me away last night—"

"You did no such thing," said Blair tenderly but wearily. "Helen . . ."

"It seems to me," Gareth said mildly, interrupting them, "that the more important question is why one of you had this idea, and why the other consented."

Helen raised her chin as she finally faced him, but he could see her hands shaking. "I am very sorry, Your Grace," she said haltingly. "I . . . that is, I had a—a change of heart. I . . . fancied myself in love with Mr. Blair . . ."

"It was the duel," Blair interrupted. "Bruton was willing to let his cousin shoot him rather than give up the girl he loved. I was his second, Wessex, and it went to my head— seeing his joy and relief when Miss Lacy threw herself into his arms . . . And when you said you would wish Bruton well, I lost my grip on reason." He gave Helen another hopeless look. "I've been in agony since the Greys arrived. I tried to forget my feelings, and I never wanted to betray you, but after the duel . . . I didn't know how I could bear to see you marry Helen."

"And running off was much safer and preferable to a duel, don't you see?" Helen pleaded. "I couldn't let him risk being shot."

"Indeed not. Blair is a capital fellow, and I would hate to see him wounded," agreed Gareth. "He's quite the most decent man I know. I congratulate you on your excellent taste."

Helen glanced at Blair in bewilderment. He seemed equally dumbstruck. Gareth wanted to shout with laughter at the look on his cousin's face.

Helen wet her lips. "But it was an abominable thing to do to you . . ."

"Not when weighed against the ills of marrying a man you could never love." He paused. "You couldn't, could you?" It was more a statement than a question, and Helen's eyes welled up again as she slowly shook her head. "Then you've done us all a great favor," he said gently. That had been his last trace of worry, that Helen might somehow have honestly regretted running off. If she had declared she was ready to carry on with the wedding, he would have had the very devil of a time.

"You're not angry?" asked Blair in disbelief. "Wessex, I . . ." Words seemed to fail him; he shook his head in stunned silence.

Gareth smiled, darted a warm glance toward Cleo. "Angry? Not at all. In fact, I have rarely been happier. And it is all due to you, Miss Grey, for having the courage to defy propriety and follow your heart. And to you, James, for going with her. My only wonder is that you came back so soon. Are you married yet?"

"No," said Blair in a dazed voice.

"Do you still wish to be?"

"Yes!" burst out Helen, which seemed to break her beloved's trance.

"The marriage contract—"

He shrugged. "I don't think we'll have any difficulty about that. Sir William, I am sure, can be made to see reason." Especially if Gareth gave him no choice.

"The guests," said Helen hesitantly.

"Oh yes, I suppose we'll have to tell them. I'll send my mother to the church." Everyone stared at him in disbelief. "If she won't go, I'll have Sophronia step in," he added. "She'd delight in calling off a wedding."

Cleo made a noise suspiciously like a smothered laugh. It made Gareth smile wider. He loved being able to make her laugh.

The runaway lovers exchanged a glance, then Blair stepped forward.

"Wessex," he said humbly. "I must apologize. You would have been well within bounds to call me out over this."

"What good would that do?" he asked, surprised. "You're my right arm, James. You might have told me earlier you had feelings for Helen, but"— he shot Cleo another glance—"in the end your timing was nothing less than perfect. Allow me to wish you great joy." He shook hands with his cousin. Helen hurried to his side, and he raised her hand to his lips. "And of course, since you're to be married," Gareth went on, "I must make you a wedding gift. A manor house, I think, somewhere nearby. You must be able to visit often."

All three of them regarded him in shock. James just nodded, his jaw working as if he couldn't speak. Helen covered her mouth with both hands, her eyes wide with hopeful joy.

Gareth clapped James on the shoulder. "I don't believe anyone else knows you've returned," he said meaningfully, "but don't take Jack's carriage this time. There's no reason to drive Hippolyta into the ground when the archbishop himself will be here. I suggest concluding your courtship in more . . . comfort."

Blair blinked a few times, then began to grin. "Wessex, I shall be in your debt forever," he said, before grasping Helen's hand and pulling her out of the room. Gareth watched them go and even raised a hand in farewell.

"That was extremely generous," said Cleo in the quiet that followed.

He nodded.

"You want them to be happy together," she said, amazed.

He nodded again.

She bit her lip. "What will you tell the wedding guests?"

He lifted one shoulder. "That I won't be marrying your sister. It's fairly simple."

She studied him. "What will your family say?"

He cocked his head to one side, a slight grin tugging at his mouth. "My mother, I expect, will be delighted. She wants me to be happy, and I would never have been happy married to your sister, as charming and lovely as she is." He started pacing toward her deliberately. "My sisters will be thrilled at the excitement of it all, particularly as they will still have Helen as a cousin. Sophronia may be put out, I grant you, at the absence of scandal and uproar, but she knew the first night that Helen and I were never meant to be."

"What did Mr. Blair's note say?" she asked, even as a soft blush stained her cheeks. "Why didn't you tell my parents when you found it?"

"Good Lord, why would I do that?" He grimaced. "Your father might have tried to do something foolish, like stop them."

"Stop them! But they were already gone—" She stopped abruptly, her eyes widening. "When did you find it?"

"Last night," he said. "About two hours after dinner. I couldn't sleep and went to my study, where James had left it. I daresay they couldn't have got much past Dorchester by then."

"Last night!" she gasped.

Gareth nodded. "I knew they would need as much time as possible to get well away. I had gone to my study to plot how I could persuade your sister to jilt me. You might imagine my relief upon discovering that she had already worked out how to do it. All I needed to do was stay quietly in my study."

She appeared unable to speak. Gently he pulled her into his arms and kissed her, loving the way her body softened against his until they fit together like two halves of a whole.

"If they hadn't run off, I don't know what I would have done," he whispered. "Do you know, I saw my place in hell waiting for me as the wedding day approached. That's what I would have earned, marrying your sister when all I could think of was you. Especially like this," he added, casting a suggestive glance down at her ripped gown.

"When?" she asked softly. "When did you start thinking that?"

Gareth shook his head. "The moment you stepped out of the carriage a fortnight ago." She looked at him suspiciously. He nodded. "Oh yes, lightning struck as you stepped out of the carriage. Toppled one of my oldest oaks to the ground, don't you remember? Split it right down the middle, and the whole thing fell. Much like my heart did when you looked at me."

"You don't believe in love at first sight!" she protested. "You said so the other day!"

"No, I don't, which is why I looked again, and again, and again, until I was quite sure I would go mad from it. I just knew." He nuzzled her neck, his mouth skimming over her collarbone and up the side of her neck. "When did you start?"

The blush that colored her face, all the way down to her

neckline, was brilliant. "Almost as soon. But of course I knew it was wrong—you were betrothed to my sister . . ."

"But not any longer." He paused. "Are you not pleased she's marrying Blair?"

"Of course I am!"

"Why?"

"Why?" she exclaimed. "Why, because they're in love!" He raised an eyebrow. "And," she hesitated only a moment, "and because if you didn't marry Helen . . ." She paused again. "Then you would be free."

"Yes."

"And—" She wet her lips. "And then it wouldn't be wrong of me to want you."

"Oh, no," he answered at once. "That would never be wrong of you. In fact, I was hoping you might keep on wanting me for the rest of your life."

Later, Cleo told herself she would remember that moment for the rest of her life. The scent of oiled leather and horses, the faint buzz of bees in the shrubbery outside the window, the morning sun slanting across the dusty floor. And Gareth, looking at her as if he had never seen anyone half so wonderful. She couldn't stop a small smile. "Is that a proposition?"

He laughed. "Proposition? My darling, I'm at an end to propositions. I made my last offer of marriage in a letter addressed to your father. May I make this one myself?" And he sank to one knee as he spoke. Cleo thought she must be goggling at him like a fool. "My darling Cleopatra," he began, then paused. "Are you truly named for Cleopatra?"

"Yes," she said dazedly. "And Helen for Helen of Troy. Father has classical fancies."

"Ah." He cocked his head to one side. "I wish I'd remembered that sooner."

"Why?" Cleo still couldn't quite take in that he was on his knees before her. Even Matthew hadn't proposed on bended knee; he'd asked her over his shop counter, which had been romantic enough, but nothing like this.

"It would have made things clearer," he said. "My parents named me Anthony, after all. Anthony never married Helen of Troy."

She cleared her throat. "He never married Cleopatra, either."

"This Anthony will," Gareth declared. "If she'll have him."

Cleo gazed down at him, his brooding dark eyes fixed on her, his thick hair still ruffled from their activities in his study. "Shall I roll myself in a rug and have myself delivered to your rooms?"

"Make certain it's a soft rug," he retorted, "for I would unroll it before the fire and not let you off it for an hour."

Cleo pretended to think. "I may have such a rug, in the shop . . ."

His eyes ignited. "That sounds like yes."

This time her smile was wide and unrestrained. "Because it is. A hundred times yes."

EPILOGUE

"**A**re you certain?" Cleo took her sister's hand.

Helen nodded. Her face was pale but determined. "I should have done it days—weeks—ago."

"I doubt it would have upset them more." Cleo shrugged philosophically, drawing a quickly repressed smile from her sister. Helen took a deep breath and opened the door in front of them.

There was a moment of stunned silence before their mother let out a peircing wail. "Helen! Oh, Helen, there you are! We were so worried—where did you go?" Her gaze flickered over Helen's dark blue traveling dress, her dusty boots, her braided hair. "Never mind that," she quickly added, as though deciding she didn't actually want to know where Helen had been. "There's still time—we must hurry!"

"Mama, there's something I need to tell you and Papa." Helen resisted her mother's attempts to drag her toward the dressing table.

"Surely it can wait!" Millicent's laughter trilled nervously. "We must get you ready for your wedding. Oh, we've barely half an hour—Rivers! Rivers, come at once!" she called for her maid.

"No, Mama." Helen glanced at her. Cleo nodded in encouragement. Her heart was racing almost as much as her sister's must be doing, but Helen had insisted that she would tell their parents. It was her wedding—at least, it was supposed to be her wedding—and she would be the one to call it off. Since Cleo had a feeling her parents wouldn't listen to a word she said anyway, she hadn't argued. "Mama, I won't marry the duke," said Helen in a clear, firm voice.

Millicent's eyes darted warily to Cleo, then veered away. "Don't be silly, dear. Your father signed the contract. You must marry the duke."

"I've already told Wessex I'm breaking our engagement," Helen went on, two bright spots of pink in her cheeks. "He took it very well."

Her mother moaned, covering her face with both hands. "Don't say that—oh, *please* don't! What will your father say?"

"Helen!" On cue, Sir William appeared in the doorway. From the set of his features, he was still toweringly angry at both daughters. "Where the devil were you?"

This time when Helen pulled against her mother's grip, Millicent let her go. "Sit down, Mama. And you, Papa."

Their father scowled, but their mother, as if sensing she would be glad to be seated when she heard Helen's news, went directly to the sofa. When Sir William didn't move in the same direction, Helen just waited, her chin up and her expression composed. Cleo went to her side without a word. Neither parent looked at her, only at Helen.

Perhaps that was to be expected. They'd said she was dead to them now, and she'd replied in kind. Still, they were her parents; it hurt that they could shut her out so easily and swiftly. And because it bothered her, she was content to let Helen break her news in any way she liked.

"You'd better have a good explanation for causing such trouble," growled Sir William, but he finally sat.

"There is something I should have told you weeks ago,"

her sister began. "Perhaps even months ago. I don't love His Grace."

Millicent blinked. Sir William scowled again. "Love? Is that why you disappeared? Some female fit of hysterics about *love* when you've got a duke waiting for you in the church?"

"You're being too hasty," Millicent cried. "Helen, dearest, you must give yourself time to fall in love with him—I don't see how you couldn't! Why, just look around at this house, this park, the lovely family—"

"I never loved him and I never could," said Helen, raising her voice slightly. "I am in love with someone else and I intend to marry him."

For a moment the silence seemed deafening.

"You can't," said her father shortly. "I've signed a marriage contract with Wessex. You're marrying him."

She shook her head. "No, Papa, I won't. He doesn't want to marry me now, either."

Her father's face reddened. "Nevertheless, he also signed that contract. It's binding!"

"Not if both of us refuse!"

Sir William made a visible effort to contain his anger. His tone softened, becoming almost wheedling. "Helen, see reason. Your marriage will be the making of us all. Wessex is a good man; your mother is right, you'll come to care for him. And you'll be a duchess. You'll be mistress of this house, dressed as finely as any of the duke's sisters, accepted in the finest circles in London. You'll never have a shop door closed in your face; your every wish can be indulged."

Helen shook her head. "It's not worth it. I am in love with James Blair, and I'm going to marry him."

Her father's eyes bulged. "The secretary? Now see here, Helen—don't be ridiculous! What sort of cork-brained idea —?" He broke off suddenly, and slowly turned toward Cleo. "This is *your* doing, putting foolish romantic rubbish into her head!"

She shook her head. "I had no idea until this morning."

"She didn't," Helen agreed. "I told no one, Papa."

A vein was pulsing in Sir William's forehead. "Helen," he said through his teeth, "I pledged my best bit of land in that marriage contract. It's the only property I've got that isn't mortgaged to the hilt. It was a stroke of luck His Grace wanted it, or else he might not have offered for you. If you jilt the duke, he could sue me for that land, ruining us all beyond redemption."

"I don't think he'll do that," Helen murmured, her lips beginning to twitch.

Cleo bowed her head to hide her expression. Gareth wouldn't sue anyone—or so he'd said, provided her father didn't make a fuss over breaking the betrothal.

"And you'd risk it, for a secretary, a man with few prospects? A man who may very well lose his position for making off with his employer's bride?" Sir William lurched to his feet. "Helen, I am ordering you: you are going to marry the duke today!"

"How can you be so willful?" wept Millicent. "How can you disdain a duke? Oh, I'd *so* looked forward to visiting Kingstag often and now we shall never be able to show our faces in all of Dorset!"

"His Grace might have you to visit, but if I were you, I'd make up with Cleo before asking." Helen winked at her. Now that she'd told her secret, she seemed uncaring of anything else. Cleo, who had carried a similar secret like an arrow in her chest, grinned back. Yes, it was very freeing to cut the lines behind her, to decide to face forward without thought for whatever dismay lay in her wake.

"Please, Helen," their mother begged. "Please reconsider. There's still time . . ."

"No, Mama, I don't think there is."

A knock sounded at the door. Cleo was already on her way to answer it. Gareth had said he'd give them ten minutes, no more.

When she'd asked if he didn't trust her and Helen, he merely raised his eyebrows in that way he had and said he didn't intend to let the wrong engagement endure a moment longer than necessary. And now, as she let him into the room, part of her almost looked forward to hearing what he intended to say.

"Your Grace!" Sir William hauled his weeping wife to her feet and bowed, scarlet-faced. "You must pardon us—a family affair—"

"Indeed." Gareth turned to Helen. "Have you told them?"

She beamed back. "Yes."

"Excellent. You'll find Blair in my mother's suite, no doubt consuming a very large breakfast. Mother thought a spot of privacy would be best."

Helen laughed. "How right she is! Thank you, Your Grace." She bobbed a curtsey and hurried from the room, leaving her parents staring after her in open-mouthed astonishment.

Gareth faced them. "Sir William, we must discuss the marriage contract."

"Er—yes. I suppose we must." Sir William licked his lips. "My daughter tells me you no longer wish to marry her. That is breach, sir."

Gareth arched one brow. "Do you intend to sue me?"

The baronet seemed to be scrambling for thoughts. "I must consider my options, sir. There was a very large settlement, you might recall—"

"Ah yes, the money that was to save you from penury, at least for a time. I have a strong suspicion it wouldn't have lasted very long. You're not a thrifty man, Sir William."

To Cleo's amazement her father turned pale. "A gentleman has expenses," he protested. "But—but if you refuse to marry my daughter, I insist on satisfaction . . ."

"Oh, I intend to marry your daughter." Gareth turned to look at Cleo, his dark eyes gleaming. "As soon as possible."

For a moment her parents stared at him, uncomprehending. Then Millicent gasped and looked at Cleo. "You?" she whispered blankly. "Cleo, dearest—"

"You want *Cleo?*" Sir William seemed to realize how appalled he sounded, and rushed on. "That is—it's such a shock, Your Grace. She's nothing at all like Helen—"

"I know," Gareth said, still watching Cleo with such heat in his gaze, she found herself blushing—and smiling so happily, her cheeks hurt. "And she suits me perfectly."

"Oh." The baronet seemed at a loss. "Well, then, I suppose I could give my consent . . ."

"Your consent?" Gareth turned back to him. "I haven't come to ask for your consent. Cleo is an independent woman of legal age. Her consent is all I need." He winked at her. "Will you still have me, darling?"

"You know I will," she told him, her pulse speeding up as she remembered having him already, up against his study door.

There was another moment of shocked silence. "Cleo," said Millicent, her voice trembling. "Cleo, darling, you'll be a duchess."

Cleo tore her eyes off Gareth and faced her mother. "I never asked for that, but since I love a duke, I suppose I shall have to endure it."

Millicent blinked, then tittered nervously. "Don't be silly, dear! You're very fortunate . . ."

"I am," she replied, giving up any pretense of not staring at Gareth with her heart in her eyes. "Even though he's a duke."

Her parents froze. Gareth laughed. "A duke in love." He glanced at the older couple. "I do apologize for any fright you might have felt when Helen went missing. I believe she was worried that her choice wouldn't be accepted calmly and reasonably, for some reason." Sir William frowned, Gareth's dry tone obviously striking home, but Millicent was too anxious to please.

"Helen's always been such a good girl! I don't know what got into her, Your Grace."

"Blair is an excellent man, and he's as deeply in love with her as she is with him," Gareth went on. "I wish them every happiness."

"And you . . . And Cleo . . ." Millicent made a helpless motion, still looking dazed. "You really want to marry Cleo?"

"Desperately." He put out his hand, and Cleo let him draw her into his arm. And to think, just a few hours ago she'd thought today would be the worst of her life . . .

Her father cleared his throat. "But the settlements . . ."

"You may have the money," said Gareth, gazing down at Cleo with a smile. "You may even keep the land. She's all I want."

There was a long moment of silence. "My," said Millicent blankly. "Oh my." She mustered a smile for Cleo. "You'll be mistress of Kingstag Castle, dear."

Cleo closed her eyes. That was the last thing she wanted to hear about. Good Lord, could her mother think of anything else?

"Indeed she will be, but I think her shop will have prepared her quite well for it." Gareth grinned. "Directing housemaids and gardeners can't be much different from directing clerks, can it, darling?"

A thought struck her. "What shall I do with the shop?" she asked him. "I can't very well run it from here."

He shrugged. "Whatever you like. Sell it, or keep it and hire a manager. I do hope you'll show it to me, though. My sisters will never let me hear the end of it if I don't take them to visit the finest, largest draper's shop in Melchester." Ignoring the way her parents were now gaping at them both, he brushed a loose wisp of hair back from her face. "Now, change out of this ghastly dress."

She struggled to keep back a laugh, wondering if her parents had noticed the damage Gareth had inflicted upon the garment.

"But Your Grace," said Millicent hesitantly. She was wringing her handkerchief and looked quite dazed. Sir William, on the other hand, looked as though he'd be sick at any moment. "What about the wedding?"

Gareth shrugged. "My mother has already set out for the church. She'll explain as much as necessary. I suggest you and Sir William compose yourself into gracious, even joyous, approval before she and the other guests return to the house." He gave her a very ducal stare. "If there is any scandal attached to this morning's events, I will hold you directly responsible. My mother couldn't have been happier when I told her how much I love Cleo, and how dearly James loves Helen."

"Oh," said Millicent again, in a very small voice. "Yes— yes, of course, Your Grace."

"Excellent." Still holding Cleo's hand, he turned and walked out of the room. In the corridor, the door barely closed behind them, he took her face in his hands and kissed her. "Thank God that's over," he murmured between kisses. "We can get on with more enjoyable things."

She laughed, winding her arms around his neck even though they were in full view of anyone coming along the corridor. Although, now that she thought about it, most of the guests would be already at the church for a wedding that wouldn't happen. They very nearly had Kingstag Castle to themselves. "Such as?"

His eyes gleamed. "This." He kissed her again. "And escape. I've never been more desperate to get out of this house and spend a day at idle pleasure."

Her breath caught. "Oh? Then perhaps . . . perhaps you might finally show me the grotto. I hear it's not to be missed . . . and quite private."

Gareth's mouth crooked in his endearing half-smile. "Anything—and everything—you want, my darling. Today and forever after."

If you enjoyed this story, please consider leaving a review online to help other readers. Thank you!

ABOUT THE AUTHOR

Caroline Linden was born a reader, not a writer. She earned a math degree from Harvard University and wrote computer software before turning to writing fiction. Since then the Boston Red Sox have won the World Series four times, which is not related but still worth mentioning. Her books have been translated into seventeen languages, and have won the NEC Reader's Choice Award, the Daphne du Maurier Award, and RWA's RITA Award.

Visit www.CarolineLinden.com to join her newsletter, and get an exclusive free story just for members.

ALSO BY CAROLINE LINDEN

THE SCANDALS SERIES

Don't miss a single scandalous moment…

LOVE AND OTHER SCANDALS

Tristan, Lord Burke isn't a marrying man—until a droll, sharp-witted wallflower starts haunting his dreams.

IT TAKES A SCANDAL

Sebastian Vane is an outcast, unfit to marry an heiress. But true love is no match for even the darkest scandal.

ALL'S FAIR IN LOVE AND SCANDAL

Douglas Bennet, notorious rake, makes a scandalous wager—which may cost him his heart.

LOVE IN THE TIME OF SCANDAL

Benedict Lennox, Lord Atherton, needs a wife—but the most likely bride is everything he never knew he wanted in a woman.

A STUDY IN SCANDAL

Lord George Churchill-Gray is an artist, not a knight in shining armor—until a runaway heiress tumbles into his arms.

SIX DEGREES OF SCANDAL

James Weston is determined to save the woman he loves—but lost— from a villain . . . and win her back in the process.

THE SECRET OF MY SEDUCTION

A scandalous author pursues her heart's desire…and makes a

thoroughly indecent proposal to her boss.

CPSIA information can be obtained
at www.ICGtesting.com
Printed in the USA
LVHW080951240223
740341LV00011B/119

9 780997 149463